THE OTHER SIDE

THE
OTHER SIDE

BY

STORM JAMESON

LONDON
MACMILLAN & CO. LTD
1946

for
Carol Hill
with affection and respect

PRINTED IN GREAT BRITAIN
BY R. & R. CLARK, LIMITED, EDINBURGH

Chapter One

JUST as he entered the house, Michel Aubrac's sister carried past him, into a room on the other side of the hall, a child who seemed to have put all the energy of its few years into growing a head that was nearly as large as its body and eyes too large for its head. Aubrac did not speak. In a moment she hurried back, she had handed the child over to someone indistinct — he had the impression of arms and a ravaged gentle face. She kissed him. Although she was younger than he was — he was thirty-five — he felt that he was holding in his arm a woman at the end of her life, so few signs were made by her body of expectancy or eagerness. But it will be a very long end, he thought, smiling ; her shoulders, thin as they were, had a hardness and lack of yielding he recognised. Their father, an old man, had these same shoulders : they were much used in the family.

She was a widow. Her husband, killed at Mézières in June 1940, had left her with just enough money to live ; she became a clerk in a warehouse in Paris, and later, with as little fuss and the same modest determination, a knot, obscure, in one of those movements of resistance to the invader which seemed at the time only an instinct of the animal body of France. Of this part of her life, so ordinary, dangerous, unlikely, she never spoke. As soon as France was freed, she went back to their father's house near Bordeaux and turned it into something between a nursery and a hospital for war orphans, taking only children who had suffered so badly during the war years that they would be a trouble in any normal community : there was the child who, by some freak of a German police sergeant, had been taken to see her parents shot, and had become deaf, and there were children who had to learn that hunger is not usual in France, and the others in whom fear, suspicion, and cunning had taken odd unchildlike forms, which had to be exorcised. There was very little money to spare, but the house was airy and comfortably shabby, and outside it the road ran through pines, and the scent of pines came into the house, with sometimes the sharp benefit of salt.

" Have you kept my room for me ? " he asked her.

" Of course."

He went upstairs and stood for a long time in the window of his room, looking across the rough garden to the trees. The brutal heat of the summer evening filled the room ; it pressed out the smells of unpolished floor-boards and old heavy pieces of furniture. He felt that behind him they were arranging themselves in some pose familiar to him as a child : if he turned round sharply he would catch the shelves at the back of his bed pushing forward his double-margined exercise books and his school copy of the *Fables* — in those days he believed that cruelty, hunger, treachery, were common form only among birds and animals — and the wardrobe door falling open would reveal darned shabby sweaters, a tennis-racket, a rod, and the leather box holding his father's top-hat. He turned. Too late — it was the room he had left in May 1940, at the end of a week's leave, and had not seen since. How carefully it had kept its innocence, of a house abandoned among pines and sand-dunes, with few neighbours — the village was three miles away, and the railway a good fifteen miles further. He congratulated it on not having seen as much as the smell of a German. Here at any rate, he thought, I can sleep.

And now to put away in this room the luggage he had brought with him — the memories of defeat, of rooms where he had spent a few uneasy nights or hours, asleep or listening for the staccato sounds — voices, footsteps — implying ruin for his hosts as well as himself; of friends whose last moments of life he carried about in him like a grimace he had forbidden himself to make, knowing too well what they would have said to him: Forget us and forget that we could not escape *them* except by dying; memories of hunger, exhaustion, cold; of moments of calm joy when he reflected that through him and the others, the few known, the many unknown, children would be born in France with clear eyes and young resolute minds. . . . He found that the room was too stubborn to accept any of these memories. Not only that — it pushed them gently to one side in his mind, claiming for itself the space they had occupied. It pushed aside, too, the images that had allowed him to live even in a Gestapo prison: corners of Paris, each of them a province, breath of the Paris Metro, breath of autumn along the Seine, signs made to him across a distance by the Paris of Baudelaire, of Abelard, of Péguy, of Picasso. You need none of these here, it told him. He agreed, and for a minute or two he walked about the room, flattering it with his hand as you flatter a horse, touching it at its sensitive points, the chipped marble of the washstand, a broken shutter — it had been broken ever since he remembered — the notches his father cut at the side of the door, measuring him against it every year until he was fifteen. How well you do your little job of being a room, he said to it: a lesson to us humans. If we were half as loyal and modest . . .

During supper, his sister asked him why he had made such a point of going to occupied Germany. "You could have been demobilised—" she smiled — "We need a man here. Father neglects the trees, he's too old and I'm too busy."

He shook his head. Although they were close friends, he could not tell her that he was going to Germany to satisfy a nagging curiosity. How is it possible that everything, in a country which has pushed to its furthest point the line of technical science, corresponds to a myth ? Why the celebrated philosopher who believes in vampires, why the doctor (known before the war, at international congresses, for his politeness and suave wit) who dreams of an asbestos room for the torture of human beings and is able, at last, to put it into operation, why the timid little tobacconist living humbly, and modestly begetting children like himself, who only knows what ecstasy is when he is ordered to die like a Niebelung, in blood and flame, with his children ? The myth of the Niebelungs, that morass of jealousy, treachery, cruelty — only words ending in *y* are orgiastic enough — springs out wherever you touch Germany, as easily and certainly as, when he touched his room, there sprang out a simple shabbiness, reasonable love of the past, of a quiet life, of peace, and a recipe for mutton with garlic. We shall never, he thought, have peace, until we know why what is common to all of us, pride and delight in cruelty, and, with a polite decency, commonly hidden, is in Germany set up as a model for school-children : they look at it and become like the young S.S. man we captured near Gex and I executed myself, after he had confessed. He died like an automaton, repeating his creed. I am sure he did his bestial cruelties with the same inhuman ardour.

These were the things he had agreed with himself not to think of. Already he felt the pain beginning round his heart. He said hurriedly :

" I have a very good reason. I can take the place in our army of occupation of a younger man — healthier. It's not pleasant, you know, in Germany. Before long, we shall lose what sense of justice and common sense we took there with us. We shall be corrupted. A pity. Nothing is too severe for the Germans. Nor too just. They could never pay for what they did here. . . . I don't think it's a job for young men — especially not for ours, we don't need to learn to hate, we shall do better if we learn how to live peacefully, with our wives." He smiled. " As for me, I'm corrupted already."

After supper, he sat in his father's room while old Emile Aubrac, lying propped up in bed, talked to him about the trees, the lack of workers, the heat, the trees, always the trees. To listen to him, you would not know there had been a war, scarcely that there had been a revolution, in France. Just as Michel was leaving him, he said :

" Time you married, my boy. We've had enough fighting. This house needs its happiness."

In his room Michel turned out the lamp and opened the shutters, to let in such air as there was in the night. There was a moon. Behind the bronzed green of the trees an immense ocean of light had engulfed everything ; there was no movement, not so much as a breath falling on it would make. It flowed into the room. Michel undressed, and when he glanced in passing it at the mirror his reflection there was rather clearer than it was usually : or was it only that the coldness of the light brought out the marks on his body ? He stood and touched one of them. Strange — but merciful — that one cannot recall agony. With a singular clearness, he recalled the mole on the face of one of the German guards. When did I notice it ? he wondered. What nonsense — and what a sight I am ! Who would want to sleep with such a gargoyle ?

In the morning when he woke, he felt the weight of the sun on his eyes before he opened them. He got up to close the shutters. Everything outside was clear, bright — and smaller and more manageable. A feeling of joy seized him, as though it had been waiting among the trees for him since his schooldays. He smiled. If I could stay here, he thought. And he imagined himself lying face-down on the dry earth under the trees, feeling his bones light and warm, and his mind empty.

When they were drinking coffee, he told his sister what their father had said.

" He is quite right," she said, smiling. " You ought to be at home and you ought to marry.'

" Look at me," he said in a light voice. " I should have to find a woman as spoiled as I am — and I shouldn't want her."

His sister gave him a look of reproach — as when they were young and he laughed at her passion for surrealist poetry : in a moment of honesty she admitted that she scarcely understood a word. . . . " You weren't always so bitter."

" I'm not in the least bitter," he said. " I'm stating a fact."

" You were not always so miserably afraid of facts."

She went away. When he was leaving to catch his train he went to look for her. He found her kneeling beside a long chair in which, rolled in rugs in spite of the heat, lay a creature half head, half skeleton. She had just succeeded in making it smile.

This time he asked her : " What is it ? "

" A child," she said firmly. " Our France. When you come on leave you'll be able to take him birds-nesting."

He spent the night at Metz. On the platform — still good-tempered after a wait of three and a half hours — he was met by the Englishman, Adrian Long, who had been attached to Colonel Maulnier's staff. They had been together in Paris for the past three months, and Aubrac was surprised, when he caught sight of Long, by his feeling of warmth. As the train drew up, Long walked beside it, blaspheming Metz in his quiet voice. There were no decent cafés, the hotel was full of tourists disguised as soldiers, and he had been cheated over his bottle of wine at lunch.

" If you hadn't arrived in time for dinner, I was going to starve," he said. " You can perhaps deal with them. I can't, I'm only an ally."

" You're an idiot," Aubrac said comfortably.

In the office in Paris he had discovered that the younger man's air of simplicity hid intelligence and a quick irony. Long was very gentle : he was also merciless for snobs, even intellectual snobs, who are common in England and are excused because they have delicate motives, and for the sellers of high-toned platitudes, who are common in France. There was a well-known writer (disguised in uniform) in the office, who practised the faults of both countries : Long had led him a frightful life until the day when he discovered him taking crumbs out of his pocket to feed the office pigeon.

With Aubrac he was always patient. He endured calmly Aubrac's worst moods, and smiled when Aubrac was as insultingly rude about the English as only a Frenchman, conscious of his from everlasting to everlasting superiority, can be. After a week or two Aubrac realised that Long was always there, attracting to himself the flow of abuse, whenever a crisis of pain pushed him beyond the bounds of excusable bad-temper. One day, after he had behaved very badly, Aubrac apologised. " My dear chap," Long said, " you can throw anything you like at me, *I* can't get you sacked." It amused Aubrac to discover that the younger man was protecting him. So much so that his temper actually improved. . . .

They left Metz in the morning. They were to report in Mainz. As their train approached what had been the frontier, Aubrac tried to seize the first moment when, in an air surcharged with legend, even the animals (hares, accord-

7

ing to a German savant, are symbols of intuition and cunning) would begin to behave irrationally. At the station before the frontier their train halted for half an hour, long enough for an old gentleman sitting on the platform to finish the top he was making for a child of six, his grandson. He invited Long, who had been giving advice from the window of the train — the English, Aubrac told him, offer advice so freely because it costs them nothing, not even their advice, since no one wants it — to take part in the inauguration ceremony. Long got out of the train, and for five minutes the other officers in it — they were all French — were treated to the spectacle of an English captain solemnly and carefully whipping a top the length of the short platform. The old gentleman was charmed.

" You can see," he told his grandson, " that the only thing you need for mobilising a top is science — and a steady wrist."

He took over the top from Long, and himself demonstrated the steadiness of his wrist. He glanced slyly at Aubrac. " Don't imagine," he said, " that I spend my life doing this. I'm a metallurgist by profession. But my grandson has never had a toy, and I insist on his having at least one. As a matter of fact, he inherited several excellent toys from his father. But in 1941 the Germans confiscated them."

" And his father ? "

" Need you ask ? " the old gentleman said softly.

Long climbed back into the train as it moved off. " I had no idea you were an expert," Aubrac said to him.

" It was my first try. I consider that it was very creditable."

Their last sight of the country of logic, rationality, and common sense, was of the metallurgist on his knees, encouraging with whoops and gestures the child's awkward efforts to keep his top upright — symbol henceforth of unshakeable constancy. In a few minutes they were in Germany.

Chapter Two

I

WHEN, in 1899, the old château of the Leyde family was burned down, Georg von Leyde rebuilt it in the form of a large square box, with a separate wing for the servants, and — except in this wing — all the modern inventions he had admired in New York. He died in 1929 and his widow did her best, fetching down from the attics pieces of furniture she had inherited and stored against this day, to bring the rooms back to a decent dignity. Had she destroyed at the same time the electric wiring, and the other proofs of her husband's bad taste, the house would not, this year, have attracted the notice of the French. The ten miles between it and Mainz, its shabby park, would probably have saved it. Or so Bertha von Leyde, scolding her married daughter, even slapping her, as Anna helped her into her clothes, said, and said it again and again, as if Anna were guilty.

When she was dismissed, Anna von Galen went downstairs. A woman of forty, she had the clumsiness of an overgrown child. She was thin, and carried herself so badly that her body seemed almost mis-shapen. In her long face — face of a middle-aged clown — her fine dark eyes gave notice, if anyone were interested, of goodness and a spark of humour.

Hesitating a little, she opened the door of a sitting-room,

where comfortable shabby leather armchairs and sofas made the best of a lamentable and disconcerting lot of nineteenth-century Gothic. The mirrors between the windows were flanked by statues of opulent young women ; the gilt had worn off, so that they seemed to be suffering from a false leprosy — it could not, in this room, be a real one. There were five windows — looking over a garden where false romanticism had been overtaken by real neglect. Anna's son, a handsome boy of twelve, dark, thin, alert, was walking restlessly about the room : he looked at his mother with impatience. Without speaking — she was a little afraid of him — she went over to a window and stood there close to the glass. She could see a large sparrow, its feathers ruffled, scurrying across the terrace. It's just been slapped, she thought, stifling her laughter. Heinrich would not forgive her if she laughed now. She started when he spoke.

" What time did they say they were coming ? "

" They didn't," she said. " All we have been told is that they'll arrive some time today." She moved from the window. " I wasn't looking for them," she said, smiling.

Heinrich stood still. " What will happen ? What was it like last time ? Tell me the worst thing you remember."

The three months after the last war during which an English mission had occupied part of the house moved very slightly in her mind under the weight of months, years, covering them. The images which should have been bright were faded ; it struck her that the young woman she could barely see was acting a part. Or why was she so serious ? Why, since she was young, did happiness not break from her in jets, as from a fountain ? Me a fountain ! she thought, smiling. I must always have been clumsy.

" The very worst ? " she said calmly. " That was the day I was walking across the lawn, past three of the English officers — it was my birthday, I was seventeen, I was trying to seem dignified, and my petticoat fell down. I had to pick it up, while they looked at the sky. It was terrible."

" Mother ! " Henrich said, outraged.

His mother only smiled. " I thought I had been disgraced for life."

" Is that all you remember ? "

" No. The day they came was like today. So clear that from the attic windows at four o'clock — I'd got up early, because it was our last free day — you could see a gleam of light, which was the Rhine, and another, which was simply the light. When I looked at it — and at our vines — I knew nothing unpleasant could happen on such a day."

" And then they came, the brutes," her son said. " Were you very unhappy ? "

She was too candid to lie to him. " No. I was very happy."

" You've forgotten," he cried.

" I remember everything that happened that year. I put my hair up, I had a white dress, and your father rode here from Mainz to stay the night. He stayed a month, and at the end of the year we were married. I liked him very much."

An expression she knew well — she thought she had noticed it first when he was a baby, before he learned to speak — crossed her son's face, a look of amused, even affectionate scorn. " And the English swine billeted in the house ? You liked them too ? "

She made one of her vague awkward gestures, half warding off his contempt, half consoling. " They weren't really much of a nuisance," she murmured. " One of them was a gardener and he gave us very good advice about the mulberries. He gave it to me. Your grandmother, of course, did not recognise them. They were polite to her. I think she amused them."

The boy made a sudden nervous movement. " Did you hear a car ? "

He is all nerves, she thought : it's not my fault, it's the war, the time, his teachers — it was the raids. But she felt guilty, as though, at some level she had not yet penetrated, she would find the evidences of her failure to protect him. And he thinks he has to protect me ! she said to herself.

" No." She put her hand out . . . impossible to reach him across the abyss separating a mother from her son who does not respect her. . . . " It won't be so bad. Nothing is incurable . . . even youth . . . you are too young."

" I hate the English," he said vehemently. " But the French are despicable. And it's the French who are coming. I can't bear it. Just to think of them living in this house with my father chokes me . . . after he has fought them twice — two wars — and both times he defeated them . . . yes, both . . . it's intolerable."

She should have been glad that he adored his father. She was glad. A thread of bitterness fastened her pleasure to her.

" Your father will know how to tolerate them."

He relaxed, becoming for a moment serene and docile. His mother did not deceive herself.

" Do you know what I remembered when I woke this morning ? I remembered the day when he burned his hand so terribly, pulling that wooden horse out of the stove for me. How old was I ? "

Often as she had answered this question —and always in the same words — Anna hesitated.

" You were three. . . . You were ill and you adored that horse."

" I haven't forgotten it," he said dreamily, " I never shall. I should think about it if the French were going to kill me, and it would help me to laugh at them."

Anna touched his shoulder. " My little love, if you want to make things easier now for your father, keep quiet, and keep out of their way."

Her husband came into the room. Paul von Galen was tall, excessively thin, with a long nose and bright pale eyes : when he smiled, which he did readily, his eyes became still brighter, almost merry, and his face, sunken, a bad colour, had a charming kindness. He was fond of pointing out that caricatures of an Englishman, of the lean stooping degenerate variety, might have been drawn from him. He stressed the resemblance by wearing shabby clothes : he wore them with a placid elegance ; even his uniforms, correct in every detail, became shapeless after he had had them on twice.

He had been very severely wounded in the war, and still limped.

" Well, Anna," he said, with warm kindness, " are you ready for them ? "

She looked at him with her strange smile, demure and sorrowful. " Yes, quite."

" They may want to take over the whole house, you know. We may have to clear out."

" Beasts, beasts," Heinrich stammered.

Galen smiled merrily. " Not at all. When I was in France I usually found it more convenient to turn the owners out of a house where I intended to live. It saves awkwardness ! "

" That's different. It was war and they had been beaten."

His father looked at him with an amused irony. " And this isn't war, and we're not defeated ? " he said, smiling. " Don't let your disappointment run away with you, my child. We need peace. Ask any woman in the village what she needs, and she'll tell you more bread, that is, peace; more soap, that is, peace; long quiet nights, a child, a husband, peace, peace, peace." His eyes danced. "Perhaps you think I'm a coward?"

The boy's indignation choked him. "I'm not an idiot."

Galen put an arm round him lightly. "Then try not to feel so blindly — it's the surest way of behaving like one."

He turned as his mother-in-law, Anna's mother, came into the room. She came in heavily, partly because she was very stout, partly to mark her annoyance. The Baroness von Leyde — she was sixty and looked older — was entirely without graces. She imposed herself on people, including the members of her family, by her lack of interest in them, and she dominated her family by her emotions as well as by her temper: other women had had as many and bitter disappointments, but they had perhaps not resented them so vividly: from her earliest childhood Anna had known that her mother was unhappy, and all that a clumsy unattractive child could do to console and amuse she had done. Her mother despised her, bullied her, and depended on her at every turn; she had agreed to Anna's marriage only on condition that her husband did not take her away, but came to live in the château. With all the fierce energy of her rages, she must, somewhere, have been weak, and one of her children, the youngest, had guessed this. The others were in the habit of being afraid of her — Anna was really afraid. Her son-in-law, perhaps, only pretended out of politeness to fear her. . . . He kissed her hand, and made a show of settling her in a chair.

"I hoped you would stay in your room," he said gently. "I told Gregor to warn me when he heard them coming, so that I could meet them in the hall and save you the pain of seeing them."

"And I have just told him to do nothing of the sort," Bertha von Leyde said drily. "You are a fool, my good

Paul. Meet them in the hall — as if they were our guests ! Let them come up here, let them feel that they are forcing themselves on a family in its own house. . . . Anna ! I told you to have the coffee here. Why haven't you done as I told you ? "

Anna made a nervous gesture. Knocking against the chairs as she went, she hurried out of the room.

" Grandmamma, I agree with you," Heinrich said eagerly.

His grandmother looked at him with some — not very much — kindness. " Oh, you do, do you ? " She drummed on the table with two fingers, and pressed her lips together — both signs of a strong displeasure. " What an incompetent muddler Anna is ! " she exclaimed. " Everything late, late."

Galen bent his head and said smoothly, " You forget, Baroness, that she runs with one servant a house which needs twenty. If you'll forgive me for saying so, it may be embarrassing for you to sit here drinking coffee while a French officer takes over the house. Let me tell Anna to bring it to you in your room."

His mother-in-law did not glance at him. " This is my house," she said, with a calm rudeness. " When I am dead, you will give orders in it, no doubt. Until then——" she closed her eyes, as though the thought that she might catch sight of him were too much.

Her tone had brought the colour to Heinrich's face. Galen was unmoved. " But you don't intend to deal with the French officers yourself, I hope ? "

" Certainly not," Bertha retorted. " That surely is your duty." She opened her eyes. " Why aren't you in uniform ? "

" An army which doesn't exist has no officers, and consequently no uniform."

He had spoken quietly, but Bertha was suddenly a very little repentant. "You must forgive me, Paul, I have a great deal to put up with. To think that they chose today to break into my house ! You have all forgotten what day it is — exactly a year since my son was killed. I have no son, he left me nothing — worse than nothing — he took with him all my happiness and my future and left me his useless wife. . . . Quite useless, since she took care not to have a child. How like a Frenchwoman to cheat us ! I warned him. My poor poor Johann."

"Mamma," Galen said gently, "you are unfair to Marie. In a very difficult position she behaves admirably."

Bertha's face darkened again. "If you think it admirable to behave like no one else, to laugh when she loses her only bracelet and cry because someone else has toothache ! She prefers raw figs, she has taught your son to dance—" here Heinrich tucked his feet under his chair — "and she can't wear even a black dress with decency."

His anger made Heinrich reckless. "Black suits her."

"That's what I said." Tired of tapping, his grandmother rested a plump fist on the arm of her chair. "She ought to be here. No doubt she has chosen today to re-make both her dresses, or turn cart-wheels in the garden. . . ."

The door opened while she was speaking. A young woman came in. She was wearing a bright cotton dress ; her hair, a skein of yellow silk fastened neatly round her head, the saffron colour of her skin and rosy cheeks, her long delicate arms and legs, all marked her as a model for young German womanhood — and no German girl of the upper classes had ever realised as well the romantic notion of a young peasant. The young man following her into the room might really have been a peasant, he was so strongly-made and swarthy, and he wore a new, shoddy, and ill-

16

fitting suit with such a self-conscious air. He looked older than his nineteen years.

At the sight of her youngest child Bertha von Leyde's face changed, its contours softened into a mask of foolish pride, and her voice sank and became caressing. . . . " There you are, my love. How nice you look." The young man approached her, she held out her hand ; he kissed it with an awkward movement, and she said graciously, " Well, Richard. Have you come to support us ? "

He had a young foolish smile. " I should like to," he said sincerely and nervously, " but I can't this afternoon. You see, my mother's alone, and she is afraid of the French. Well, not afraid, but she wants me to be there."

" I don't think they'll trouble you," Bertha said.

" No, I don't think they will," Richard said, with simplicity. " But I have put on my only decent suit in case."

Heinrich giggled. " Do you expect to be presented ? "

Richard Gauss looked at the boy with a confused anger. He recognised the malice, but he did not know how to deal with it. His visits to the family were an agony, lightly modified by his better opinion of himself since Lotte's mother accepted him, the son of the village chemist, as a suitable husband for Lotte von Leyde, and, too, by that detachment he had learned during his six months in the Air Force, always surprised when he stepped from his machine to find his life waiting for him, a good little bitch, where he had left it. All that had been easier, because he had trained for it, than walking into this room. And yet he knew he had the right to be here. It was his body which didn't know.

Colonel von Galen was speaking to him in his soft good-humoured voice. " You're quite right, Richard. We must do our best without uniforms to look as though we can survive defeat."

Richard was speechless with gratitude. And he could only look sheepishly at Bertha von Leyde when she said,

"Your mother is lucky to have her son, Richard."

Anna von Galen had come in. She stood holding the tray awkwardly against her body — it might have been bent into this shape only to support trays. She said quietly,

"You still have a grandson, mother."

"I hadn't forgotten," Bertha said. "I expect a great deal of him." She added, with malice and self-pity, "I must try not to expect too much, my life has had many disappointments."

Lotte seized her chance to punish Heinrich — it was an old feud, begun when, an infant, he defended himself against her tyranny — "Since you've nothing else to do, you might earn your living as a jockey."

It was too cruel and unexpected a gibe. Only Lotte would have made use of the grief Heinrich had felt the day he knew he would not be going into the army, there was no longer an army, there was scarcely even a Germany. Tears of rage came into his eyes before he could stop them.

"It's not my fault if my mother waited twelve years to have me!"

With trembling hands his mother set the tray on a small table. Her voice, too, trembled, and was almost inaudible. "Your fault was to be born into a house where everything a child wants had already been given away to another child."

"What nonsense!" Bertha said angrily. "Your child had everything he needed, he had only to ask you for a thing and you gave it to him. And you seem to have forgotten the day Lotte chased a ferret away from his cradle. She was only eight!"

"I never said she wasn't brave," Anna said, quietly

obstinate. " She's very brave. But she was unkind to him."

" Poor little innocent ! " Lotte jeered.

" Must you clatter the cups like that ? " Bertha asked her elder daughter. She turned to Lotte with a fond smile. " You needn't be here when they come, my love. You and Richard go."

Lotte was indignant. " Good heavens, I came back on purpose. We don't know what sort of brutes they are. They might arrest us."

Anna, who was pouring the coffee, went on pouring into the same cup. Her son noticed it in time to save her from disaster : he took the pot from her deftly and without a word, and poured for her. She smiled at him timidly.

" I'd rather you weren't arrested," Bertha said. Her eyes implored the girl to go away.

Lotte took no notice. " They can arrest me, they can shoot me," she said gaily, " if they like — if that's all they know how to do." She was looking at herself in a mirror : her glance was caught by an object on the semicircular table backed against the glass. She picked it up. " Why is Johann's miniature here, mother ? Has Marie got tired of keeping it under her pillow ? "

" I told Marie to bring it down," Bertha said drily. " She had no right to keep it in her room."

" It is hers," Anna murmured.

" Johann belongs to us all," Bertha said with a melancholy dignity. " And where is Marie ? " she said in a sharper voice. " I shan't allow her to evade meeting her countrymen — they murdered my son. I believe her to be heartless, but she is the wife of a dead German soldier, and for once she must behave like one. Anna, run upstairs to her room and fetch her down."

Anna stood up. As if she had decided that nothing could make her situation worse, she said,

"Perhaps she doesn't want to meet the people who killed her husband."

"I heard her singing this morning," Lotte said, with malice.

The door opened before Anna reached it. The French daughter-in-law came in. She was wearing a black dress, but by merely adding to it a white collar and white cuffs she had given it an air of lightness, as though she wanted to say : I am in mourning but you need not condole with me, it is my business, not yours. Or : You can look the other way when I am crying ; look at my collar. She was thin, and dark, very dark — but if you ran your fingers through her hair you would think you were holding them in the light. She had a quick light step. She kissed her mother-in-law's hand with smiling ease, as though sure that she were approved. Bertha said coldly, "Well, Marie, you've decided to come down ? "

Marie smiled. "This is the only collar I have left, and I had to iron it."

"I see you intend to fascinate the dear French," Lotte said to her. "I suppose you know what will please them."

' Yes, I do. . . . It would please them to find us shabby and broken-down. I hope they will be very disappointed to see that air-raids and hunger only made us elegant." She paused, and said with a simple friendliness, "You must have had the same idea yourself. You look lovely, doesn't she, Richard ? "

"He thinks I ought to have made myself repulsively ugly," Lotte cried.

Marie lifted her eyebrows. "Why ? "

Regretting that she had given herself and Richard away, Lotte said carelessly, "I daresay Johann would have said the same things to you."

"Johann ? " Marie said lightly. "Oh, no, he liked me

best when I was feeling happy. But, you know, I was never anything else, it made me deliciously happy to watch him yawn, or drink his coffee. Dear Johann."

" Dear Johann ! " her mother-in-law echoed, savagely indignant. " Poor Johann, if he had been here today."

" We should have been here together," the girl said, smiling.

Paul von Galen spoke before Bertha could form the sentence he saw rearing itself on her tongue. " My dear Marie, you won't be responsible for anything unpleasant that may happen, your marriage has made you as German as the rest of us, and you'll share all our penalties. I'm sure you feel them as severely as we do."

Grateful for his kindness, Marie did not choose to show it. She smiled. " Thanks for the penalties."

For some moments Richard Gauss had been forming in himself the courage to come forward and take his leave of the baroness. He did it clumsily, blushing.

" I'm afraid I must go now," he said, with an assurance that sounded false in his own ears.

Lotte gave him a bright angry glance. " Must you ? Your mother doesn't need you, you'd better stay with us." With me — since I ought to be more important to you than your mother, her glance warned him.

The young man looked at her. " I promised her I'd go back." Don't scold me before your family.

" It's ridiculous," she said loudly and firmly. " Besides, for all you know, the French may arrest us."

This idea sharpened the anguish he felt in opposing her. " Lotte, I must go," he mumbled.

She turned her back. " All right. Go."

He stumbled over his feet in his misery and embarrassment, but he went. As the door closed Heinrich began the speech he had been meditating :

" Lotte, you always said you were going to marry a rich man, and do just as you liked. It's not quite the same thing to fall for a sort of shopkeeper — he would have been a shopkeeper if he hadn't been able to go into the Air Force." He had an inspiration. " And he doesn't even let you bully him. Although he's a year younger than you are."

Lotte kept her temper. " So you don't approve of him ? What a blow for Flight Lieutenant Richard Gauss that little Heinrich von Galen doesn't like him."

" I like him very much," Heinrich said. His eyes sparkled. " But I don't think you ought to let him wear yellow shoes. Not even with his only decent suit."

" Don't talk like that about him," she cried, forgetting herself in a loyal fury. " He's a hero."

" He is a thoroughly nice boy," Marie said, " which is better."

" He doesn't need anyone's good opinion," her young sister-in-law said coldly, " least of all a foreigner's."

Anna had been looking out of the window. She turned round. " They're here," she said in a quiet voice.

There was a moment's silence, broken by Bertha von Leyde. " This really is the most detestable coffee I ever drank. Is it turnip or dandelion ? "

She looked from face to face, inviting them to admire her coolness. It did not last. Looking at Lotte, she trembled and pulled with her fingers at the high neck of her bodice. Then the steps of at least half a dozen persons sounded in the hall below this room. Two sets of footsteps detached themselves from the rest and mounted, slowly, the stairs.

Marie opened her eyes widely, as though without this effort they would have closed themselves. The others had turned away from it but she faced the door, and she was the only one who saw it opened by old Gregor — who had bent himself double — and the two officers come in. She was prepared for anything, any shape of enmity — except for this skeleton of a body, these scarred lashless eyes lifted above a sharp point of irony, this derisive bitterness in victory. What hope she had nursed, of being able to touch her country, was it with the tip of a finger, died. This Frenchman walked as though he were recovering from an illness, with obvious pain, yet it would be impossible to feel sorry for him. He is unforgiving, she said to herself. She saw that the other officer was English ; he was serious and pleasant, but there was little kindness in his manner, as little as in the Frenchman.

It was the French officer who spoke. " Major Aubrac."

In his quiet voice Galen said, " I am Colonel von Galen."

" You are the owner of the château ? " Aubrac asked. He spoke admirable German.

Galen made the formal gesture of presenting Major Aubrac to the baroness. " The house belongs to my mother-in-law, Baroness von Leyde—" the French officer saluted stiffly, and was ignored — " but you will let me act for her. Would you prefer to speak French ? I am fairly fluent, I was in France for four years."

" Really ? " Aubrac said, in a flat dry voice. " We'll speak German."

" Since you prefer it," Galen said with his gentle half-smile.

Aubrac sat down — the English officer remained standing. " As you have been notified, the château is required by the military authority. We shall not come in until the day after tomorrow, so you have twenty-four hours to make your arrangements."

" It is a large house, and my mother-in-law is an old

lady whose son has been killed. We hoped you would not need to take the whole house."

" I regret," the Frenchman said indifferently.

Galen did not drop his resolute air of being the host in a friendly gathering. " After all, there are forty-nine rooms, and eight more in the servants' wing." He smiled. " We have no servants, of course, except the old man you saw, who was my mother-in-law's father's coachman."

How is it possible to be rude to a man who makes you free of his relations by marriage ? Aubrac managed it easily. Looking at the English officer, and ignoring Galen, he said,

" Captain Long, you might look round the house now. . . . Be good enough to take this officer through the house," he added, without turning his head to look at Galen.

" If you will let my son take you round," Galen said gently. " Heinrich. . . ."

As he came forward, Heinrich arranged his face into a mask of reserve and hate. Captain Long looked at this poor young mask with a gentle amusement; he took care not to show it, and remained grave when the boy came stiffly to attention before him and announced himself. " Heinrich von Galen. Please come this way."

He opened the door they had come through. The Englishman thanked him casually, and they went out. As she watched them, Marie felt that she must, or she would disgrace herself by laughing or crying, upset this ceremonious parade — how ridiculous men are ! Glancing at the women, she saw that even Anna had forgotten to be herself : but she had become all grief where the other two were all contempt and hatred. Major Aubrac was leaning back in his chair, indifferent. She walked towards him with a friendly smile.

" Wouldn't it be possible," she said lightly, " for us to

24

keep the servants' wing ? It's quite apart from the rest of the house. Let me show you." She crossed the room with her quick step, and opened the door on the left — it was not a door, it was a section of the panelling. Without moving from his chair, Aubrac turned his head and watched her. That was already a point. She held the door widely open. " You see — there is this landing, and the door at the other side leads to the servants' rooms. Of course they have their own outer door, on to the yard. And there are, you know, the barns and stables. If you object to our living under the same roof, you might perhaps let us live there ? "

Aubrac looked at her. " Why ? "

" Why not ? " she said, smiling. " You are not turning us out merely for the pleasure of making another family homeless — we should, you know, be homeless, since all the houses in the village have already four or five families of bombed-out from the towns, and you can see for yourself that we shall not fit easily into one room." In spite of herself her voice became mocking. " Being defeated has not made us want to live in each other's arms. We hear a great deal about our duty to civilise ourselves — I hope you won't imagine that it can be done in this way. Believe me, you will be terribly disappointed."

Aubrac had risen from his chair — perhaps reluctantly, certainly with a twinge of pain. He spoke for the first time without an inhuman formality.

" There would be no need for anyone to cross this landing ? "

She had the sense that her mind was stretching itself ; the bandages had been taken off and it could use its muscles freely and easily. I must be careful, she thought. But no one who suddenly regains the use of a limb can help using it, and with delight.

" It leads nowhere, except to the servants' wing. This château was built to house two sorts of human beings. It could hardly be more up to date."

" After all, why not ? " Aubrac said, as if to himself.

He looked into Marie's face again. She made a light gesture of relief, hiding her triumph.

" Thank you, you are very kind."

He may have been annoyed with himself. Turning from her sharply, he said, " The persons living here are all members of your family ? "

" Yes, all," Galen answered. " My wife. My sisters-in-law, Frau Captain von Leyde, Fräulein von Leyde—" delighted to be able to show defiance, Lotte turned her back, showing a smooth young nape and elbows still as rough as a child's — " and my son. Six persons."

" Seven," Marie said. " You're forgetting old Gregor."

" I had, yes, forgotten him. He's not exactly a member of the family."

" You can include him," Aubrac said drily. He seated himself again. " Please be out of this part of the house by this time tomorrow."

" I'm immensely grateful to you." Paul von Galen smiled. " If I may say so, it's the first time since the war that I've felt certain of being able one day to talk to a Frenchman as though we were both soldiers, without having to remind myself all the time that I am a Boche."

Looking in front of him under his scarred eyelids, Aubrac said with calm bitterness, " I'm fortunate, I find that no effort."

Bertha von Leyde had been listening with a face which became gradually more congested. She blew up at this point. " Aren't you ashamed of yourself, coming here with your vile habits — and for the second time ? "

" You can reassure yourself, madam," Aubrac said,

without looking at her. " We've learned no new habits, not even during the last five years."

Before she had time to reply, the English officer came back with Heinrich. He looked at Aubrac with an obvious anxiety. Dragging himself from his chair, Aubrac said,

" You've looked at everything ? Right. We'll go."

Anna, speaking with her natural gentleness and simplicity, interrupted him. It was the first time she had moved since the officers came in, and her interruption had all the effect of a door breaking, or of a child who begins to cry in the middle of a scene between his parents. Everyone looked at her, and everyone felt guilty — even Aubrac. And even Marie — who felt ashamed suddenly of her cleverness.

" There's one thing — I've always made my own polish for the furniture, from bees-wax, you know. It's better for it than anything you can buy. Would you let me give you some — for the men to use ? "

Aubrac looked at her for a second, and answered her with what was almost kindness. " We shall put some of the things out of the way. That certainly—" he waved his hand at a large piece of furniture ingeniously carved to represent the front of a cathedral, with a single tower ; below the spire a great many niches held, in the place of statues, birthday mugs, fans, Easter palms, and pottery bearing the arms of German cities — " By the way, what is it ? " he asked.

Anna smiled at him indulgently. " Why, a cupboard. It belonged to my grandmother. It is a copy of Strasbourg Cathedral. As you can see."

" A copy . . ." Aubrac murmured. His face twitched. " I see no reason why you shouldn't keep it. . . . I'll have it carried to your rooms."

" That's very kind of you," Anna said.

Yes, yes, Marie thought, with anger, you can enjoy your irony at her expense. Phrases with which to mock his pretence of generosity sprang into her mind, but before she could speak, Bertha von Leyde had turned furiously on poor Anna.

" Kind — to let you keep a piece or two of my furniture ! " she raged. " You might thank him at the same time for letting me keep my clothes."

Aubrac ignored her. Hesitating as he walked past one of the mirrors, he picked up the miniature of Johann von Leyde — " You can take personal things of this sort with you," he said, dropping it again on the nearest chair. Marie gave a cry of horror and ran forward.

" Oh, be careful, be careful."

In the same moment, she realised her blunder and pressed the back of her hand to her lips. . . . Aubrac halted beside the chair.

" Ah, you speak French ? " he said. " You speak it very well."

" I was born in France," she said quietly.

He examined her with as much insolence as can be conveyed simply by withdrawing all kindness, all decent reserve, from the back of the eyes. " Really ? A German born in France. How very interesting."

She was silent.

" Oh, I see," he said. " You had the bad luck before the war to marry a German."

" I married in 1942," she replied.

His manner became polite — a politeness under which she had the greatest difficulty in breathing. " Forgive me," he said, " I had no intention of exposing you. It was stupid of me."

So clear an intention to humiliate gave her back her strength and composure. " May I have the miniature ? "

she asked serenely. She became aware that the Englishman, at a little distance from both of them, was watching her attentively.

Aubrac picked it up. She stretched out her hand, but — for fear that he might touch it — he handed the miniature to Captain Long.

" Give this to Frau von Leyde."

2

The kitchen, a large room with an immensely high ceiling, had no windows : the light came from the skylight in the centre of the ceiling, and a conscienceless servant, hoping to waste a minute by looking outside, would need a ladder or the agility of a monkey. There were two doors : one, broad enough to allow a servant to walk through carrying the widest possible tray, led to the main wing ; the other, a single narrow panel at the head of three stairs, to the servants' bedrooms, and also into the yard. Floor, table, dresser, chairs, were strewn with a variety of things fetched from the main wing. All four women and Heinrich were getting in each other's way and making confusion worse by dragging objects from underneath a pile to lay them on the top of another.

Marie noticed suddenly the Germanness of the things in the room. It struck on her eyes and her other senses as though she had just stepped on to the quay in a foreign country after a long voyage, or as though they had been keeping their backs to her and had all at once turned round, with that malignity of inanimate objects — they wait for the right moment to show their dislike. Or it may be, she thought, I'm seeing them as they would look to that man Aubrac. This vexed her intolerably. She seized a heap of towels and shook it. The vase they had been hiding rolled on to the floor, and broke. Bertha von Leyde started and groaned.

" This is too much," she said angrily.

Anna stumbled towards her. " I'll help you to your room, mother."

Bertha waved her aside. " Lotte will help me, won't you, my little love ? I need help to begin a life of poverty and disgrace."

She leaned heavily on Lotte as she climbed the three stairs, an admirable performance of a woman crushed by misfortune. The others dared not smile, but she had no sooner gone than the room, which had been dull, filled with sunlight. She must have been standing on the jet. . . . Heinrich threw himself into a chair ; his mother came to stand near him, with her pitiful smile, her arms hanging at her sides, all the air of a servant who is on friendly terms with the family. Marie made a gesture of relief and joy, then ran to the dresser and began turning over the things flung there.

" My nail scissors, Anna, where did you put them ? I can't begin a life of disgrace without nail scissors. Besides, I brought them from home."

" In my room — I'll get them," Anna said. She did not move. " It's not going to be so bad," she murmured. " After all, they were reasonable."

" Very reasonable," her son cried. " They left us our rags. The French are swine. . . . I'm sorry, Marie."

" Oh," Marie said calmly, " when he dropped Johann's miniature the only bit of France still holding out in me—" she touched it — " my ear — surrendered. I am a German."

Anna von Galen's smile became gentler and more tragic. " And that was why you spoke French ? " She went down on her knees to pick up the pieces of the broken vase.

" That was only a child who had been listening. She won't speak again," Marie said, laughing.

" Only every time you move," the German woman said tenderly, " and when you are asleep."

Marie watched her without helping — who ever thought of offering to help Anna with a tiresome job ? " You'll never know how much I love you," she said. " I can talk to you without being afraid — you don't suspect me of cleverness."

Heinrich jumped up and ran to her. " You can to me ! "

" Don't imagine I'm unhappy here. I'm very — perfectly — happy. . . . If you believe Lotte, that proves I'm an egoist and quite useless."

Anna had laid the broken vase at the back of a shelf — it would lie there in state for a few days : she could never bring herself to throw a thing out at once. Now she was searching everywhere, with a gentle distraction — for what ? She spoke without turning her head.

" That's what I admire in you — you've always refused to be unhappy. You had every excuse . . . living in a country which doesn't like or respect happiness."

" Mother, what on earth are you looking for ? " Heinrich said impatiently.

Anna turned from the cupboard, smiling. " I've found it ! My birthday mug, Heinrich."

The boy laughed unkindly. " I suppose you would sooner have lost the war."

" But since we've lost the war . . ." she murmured. She held the mug between both hands. " No one told me when I was born that I should have to keep Germany alive through a second war. . . . I've always known that my job was to look after all the things we use in the family. My only way of remembering my grandmother is to polish her cupboard. . . . When your wife asks me for this cup for her first baby, I shall thank her for making me very slightly immortal." She freed one hand, to touch Marie's arm, clumsily and timidly. "You don't hear what any of these things of ours say, Marie." She blushed. "It's not your fault," she went on hurriedly. "They talk about people you never knew, and only in German. . . . I wish they would bring the Strasbourg cupboard. . . . I'm so afraid. He might easily decide to keep it — I don't suppose he has ever seen anything like it."

This was too much for her son. "Oh, let him steal it," he shouted. "Why keep anything that reminds you of Strasbourg? I should like to destroy it — and Strasbourg — and France. And Germany. And your birthday mug." He was beside himself, as they say — but neither of his selves looked at the other. "If only I could destroy everything — so that everyone was helpless, and without a future. I hate everybody."

His mother looked at him sorrowfully. "You are too young."

He was half ashamed of himself. "My poor dear, you don't understand anything," he mumbled.

"You're talking nonsense," Marie said lovingly; "the one thing they can't forbid us is the future, they can't make you short-sighted or squinting, or cowardly or a liar. You have every chance to live for a hundred years. What more do you want? I wish Johann had just five years of your future. Or one! Or five minutes! In five minutes I could live a long happy life with him."

"You always know what to say to me," the boy said. He went to his mother and put his arms round her. "I'm a fool," he said. "I'm sorry. Give me something to do."

"You can come with me to the village," Anna said joyously. "We shall have to pass the sentries, and I'm a little — no, not nervous — but how do you pass a sentry

in your own garden ? Ought I to say good-morning to him ?
It's really a problem."

Does she make a clown of herself so that he will laugh ?
Marie wondered. No, she is really simple. Heinrich
laughed.

" The French are very democratic," he said ; " you
needn't do more than kiss his big toe."

When she was alone, Marie went quickly to the shelf
above the stove and took down the miniature. The night
before, when she was thinking of her husband, as she
always did after she had prayed for him, the image of him
that came was that of the miniature, smiling and anonymous.
He is leaving me, she thought ; he prefers his family. She
fell asleep on this desolate idea. Now she tried to outstare
the heartless fixity of these eyes : they had destroyed the
living memory as firmly as a death mask fixes for ever the
image not of a life but of death.

She heard someone coming and replaced it carefully,
and seated herself behind a table piled high with linen
which she began to sort. The door opened very gently.
It was Richard Gauss. He came into the room, awkward
in his anxiety to please. He was wearing, Marie saw, the
new shoes. To give himself confidence.

" Good morning, Frau von Leyde."

" Did you pass our sentries ? " she asked gaily.

" No. I came through the stables."

He sat down and looked moodily at the floor. Something has upset him so badly that he is not even nervous,
she thought. After a moment she asked him what was
wrong.

" Nothing," he said. " One of their big planes is just
going over. I couldn't bear to watch it."

She smiled to hide her pity. " Poor Richard. But don't
worry. They'll let you fly again one of these days."

" Yes. Safe easy commercial planes," he said heavily.
" No thank you."

" Oh, Richard — even you ? " she cried.

" What have I said ? "

" Must you have danger, and I suppose glory, to enjoy
flying ? "

" I don't know what you mean. . . . I want to have
something powerful in my hands, something you can feel
a pleasure in handling." He laughed shortly. " You
needn't repeat it to anyone."

He had not heard Lotte come noiselessly into the room.
She said sharply, " What is she not to repeat ? " His face
changed as though its blunt, rather heavy features had lost
one thickness of flesh suddenly ; his blue eyes became
serene — so much serenity can one harsh voice bring when
it is also clear and young. He jumped up.

" Oh, Lotte. . . . I came to tell you that it's all right,
they've taken me, and I start work tomorrow. . . . If only
I don't make a fool of myself," he added ruefully.

" Why should you ? "

" Well, I'm not very quick, you know, and I suppose a
clerk ought to be, even in a village station."

In a minute I'll go out and leave them, Marie thought.
She glanced up from her sorting to ask with an air of
interest, " A railway clerk ? "

" Why shouldn't he manage a railway ? " Lotte said
defiantly. " It's a perfectly decent job."

Richard's honesty ruined her — not for the first or last
time.

" I shan't be a manager exactly, Lotte. What worries
me is the salary. Do you think you can possibly live on
it ? "

In her anxiety to comfort him, she ignored her sister-
in-law. " Silly boy, it's more than enough for two people

as sensible as we are," she said, with her mother's fierceness.
" We'll get married at once."

" I'm not sensible about you, I want you to have everything and be happy."

" I have everything."

Marie could not move. She was afraid to break the
current joining them — almost visible ; they were drawn
closer together by it, and stood, not daring to touch each
other, held on the edge of the precipice by fear, by a terrible
happiness.

" Are you sure ? " Richard asked under his breath.

" I'm sure we can live in one room as if it were a palace,"
Lotte said, " and when we have a palace — and ten children
— it will seem like one room. Don't you believe me ? "

" I believe anything you say."

Lotte moved away sharply ; she had remembered that
Marie could hear them. " What were you telling Marie not
to repeat ? "

Marie looked down at the table and said casually, " We
were talking about flying."

Lotte turned very red : she hated him to be reminded
of the Air Force — his life in it had absorbed him, and she
was afraid for him and jealous. " If you were still in the
Air Force I wouldn't marry you," she said loudly.

" Why on earth not ? " he said, astonished. " You liked
me in the uniform."

" I should never have a happy moment. I want to be
sure of you. If you are safe and wearing an old jacket,
which I shall have to mend, I shall like you much better
— though I detest mending. Why do you want to get
killed ? "

" I don't."

" I should have thought you had enough in your six
months — and when you knew it was hopeless. . . ." She

frowned. " It can't have been pleasant."

" It was unpleasant, I was afraid all the time," Richard said slowly, " and I was happy. And in fact if we'd been winning I shouldn't have been half so happy. It was just the absolute certainty we had of being outnumbered, out-gunned — almost, except that we were alive — out-lived — that made it right."

Marie looked up. She could not help it ; she wanted to catch on Richard's face the light that this sudden avowal — it was that — must have made on it. No, he had still his face of an honest and simple young man — of a chemist's son, Heinrich would say. But it is only these, and a few poets, who make real avowals : people of importance, people who get on in the world, powerful people, are discreet. . . . I ought to hold my tongue, she thought. She said eagerly,

" Explain that to Heinrich, Richard. It's dangerous at his age to feel humiliated. If you could get it into his head that the glory — oh, and the tragedy, too, but that's less important — the glory always goes over to the weaker side . . . it did to France and England in 1940 and now to us . . . you would save him."

Richard turned to her gratefully. " That's exactly what I mean."

Marie frowned at him, so that, disconcerted, he would turn back. She was too late. Vexed, Lotte was saying harshly, " Well, you'd better go. Mother thinks you come here too often, you'd better not come for a few days."

Now he was disconcerted. Smiling awkwardly, he made for the door. " Good Lord, I'm sorry," he stammered. " I thought I was getting on rather well with her."

Lotte made a show of hurrying him across the room. " Never mind. It's all right." In the doorway she threw her arms round him with a childish ardour, pushed him

out, closed the door on him, and came back into the middle
of the room with an air of jaunty assurance.

Marie looked at her with a smile. " Why did you tell
him that silly lie ? Now he'll feel more awkward here than
ever."

" That doesn't matter," Lotte said in a defiant voice.
" I won't let you corrupt him."

" You don't know what you're saying."

" I know very well, thank you," Lotte retorted. " You
have no conscience, you mix up pleasure and duty, just as
you mix up defeat and victory, until it seems as if nothing
matters except to be enjoying yourself. Richard and I are
going to be happy, but not in your easy way."

" You think it so easy ? " Marie lifted her hands in a
gesture that might have been indifference. She was silent
for a moment, then she said softly, " You love Richard
very much, don't you ? "

Lotte looked at her with mistrust. " Why shouldn't I ? "

" Yes, why not ? He's very honest, and loyal — and
kind. . . . The only thing the world needs is kindness.
With a little more of it we could do without politics and
politicians and conferences and the rest. . . . You're very
wise to marry Richard. He's simple and he has so much
goodness."

She had meant what she said, but as she said it she
knew it would please Lotte, and that for a moment the other
girl would trust her.

" Yes, hasn't he ? " Lotte said eagerly. " He's much
better than I am. If I hadn't met him in time I should have
become impossible — bad-tempered and bored, like my
mother."

" Then why do you bully him ? "

" Oh, it doesn't hurt him, you know — he likes it, it
makes him feel safe to quarrel with me, because when it's

all over, there we are as if we'd grown together. That's
what I like. I should hate a husband I had to be gentle
with—" she laughed as noisily as a boy — " So dull !
Richard and I quarrel terribly, it's one of our ways of
agreeing with each other." Her eyes sparkled. " One of
our more exciting ways."

Marie forgot that she must always be on guard. " Yes.
. . . Perhaps Jeannot—" she hesitated — " it's not easy
to live in this house — perhaps I should have made him
feel safe. I wonder."

" What used you to call him ? " Lotte asked.

" Jeannot," Marie repeated softly.

Lotte sat down at the table. She had become gentle.
" What was it like ? Were you terribly in love ? I can't
imagine it with Johann."

" I don't know." Marie smiled. " You see, we never
quarrelled. It wouldn't have done, we had different ideas,
different languages, we hadn't even the same way of eating
bread. . . . I used to watch Jeannot as though he were a
child. My first child."

" Poor Marie," Lotte said gently.

But Marie refused the offered pity as firmly as she had
always refused to pity herself. " Don't be sorry for me,"
she cried lightly. " We had two years, and we knew
every moment of them, that it wouldn't last, one of us
would be killed." She hesitated, and went on without
thinking — Lotte's kindness had given her a false confidence — " And as Richard says, you live a long marvellous
life in the last two minutes."

Lotte's face changed. " When did he say that to you ? "

I have made her jealous, Marie thought sadly. She tried
to save herself by answering carelessly, " I forget . . . one
day he came here and you were out."

Lotte spoke with the jeering malice of a schoolgirl. " I

don't know why he confides in you. Perhaps he believes you were heartbroken when your dear Jeannot was killed. . . . Jeannot ! " She mimicked Marie's voice. " What a fatuous name. . . . You don't look as though you'd suffered. You don't show a sign ! "

" Oh, you think my arteries ought to have hardened, and I should have turned yellow ? " Marie said, smiling. " What a simple idea you have of despair. I hope you'll never have to change it."

She had moved towards the door while she was speaking : though she defended herself, she never allowed one of these scenes to become a quarrel — that would make her life here impossible, as well as disgrace her in her own eyes. . . . She had not reached the door. It opened, and Anna came in.

A grey tinge had come into the pallor of her face ; she might have been walking in her sleep, she had that air of moving her body about like a burden. In a flat quiet voice she said, " Heinrich has been arrested."

Lotte jumped up. " Anna ! " she said, almost with anger. " What do you mean ? "

" We were coming home across the park," her sister said in the same voice ; " three soldiers came out on the terrace carrying the Strasbourg cupboard, and Heinrich rushed at them and asked them why they were stealing it. They didn't understand him, of course, and laughed at him, and he struck one in the chest. They dragged him into the house and I tried to go with him—" she moved one hand very slightly — " they drove me off."

Lotte turned on Marie. " You see what your friends are like ! " she shouted. " I knew we ought to have left the house."

Marie looked calmly into her face. " Do you hate me because I was once French, or because I married your brother ? " She walked quickly to Anna and said in a gentle voice, " Anna my dear, don't be afraid, the French are not cold devils, they lose their tempers quickly, far too quickly, but it doesn't last : they'll release Heinrich, he's a child."

" Don't they punish children in France, then ? " Anna said swiftly.

" Not for such a trifle."

Anna did not move. " He's not a timid child. He'll give them plenty of excuse."

" I wish I'd seen him hit the beast—— " Lotte stopped sharply. Followed by Paul von Galen, the baroness had come into the room. She had caught Lotte's words. " What were you talking about ? " she asked, already crimson with nervous emotion.

No one answered her. Lotte looked at her sister, but although she struggled with herself, her lips moving, Anna did not speak. Plainly she could not. Her mother realised that she and not Lotte was in trouble, and opened her mouth to treat the clumsy creature as she deserved. Marie tried to attract the lightning to herself.

" Heinrich. He and Anna were crossing the park and he quarrelled with one of the soldiers, and struck him, and — they took him into the house."

" Anna ! " Bertha von Leyde screamed. She ignored Marie. " What were you thinking about to take the boy near them ? You must have been mad. How could you be such a fool ! " She flung her arms up. " Now what's to be done ? We must act at once — at once. Paul, you must go and see them. Explain that Anna is a fool, and bring the boy back — before they ruin him."

Paul von Galen took no notice of her. He had paled a little — that is, his cheeks became more sallow, and the end of his long thin nose became red — but he was calm. He spoke to his wife as though he were trying both to protect her — from her mother — and comfort her. Yet she flinched.

" Don't worry, my dear. You'll get one of your head-aches and be fit for nothing. We'll get the boy home — and I'll punish him myself." He forced himself to smile. " What was it all about ? "

Anna looked at him. " They were taking the Strasbourg cupboard — stealing it . . ." she began.

" And you let him get into trouble for that ? " her mother interrupted. " Fool, fool ! " Tears of rage sprang to her eyes. " First Johann and now Heinrich. He isn't my son, I only had one son, and with the way you spoil him he may never be much good, but he's the only grandson — and you must risk his life for a cupboard ! "

" Mother, I—— " Anna said in a low voice. She stopped. She turned her face from her mother to her husband, like a dog appealing from the master who beats him to the master who only watches. Moving stiffly and awkwardly, she stepped backwards to the side of the room, and stood there, arms hanging, as if the distance separating her from them was too wide for her to attempt to speak.

" I ought to have forbidden him to cross the park," Galen muttered. " They couldn't help arresting him, I should have done it myself. . . . I wish it hadn't happened."

Marie had been watching him. " You're anxious," she said quietly.

He shook his head. " No."

" It will be that hideous deformed major," Lotte said to her spitefully, " the one you tried your charms on. . . . The French are awful. Fancy making a cripple an officer ! " She laughed loudly. " He put *you* in your place, my girl."

Galen looked at her sternly. " Lotte, you are very young and silly. I hope Marie has more sense than to be hurt or offended."

Marie smiled. " I'm two years older than Lotte, and

41

you don't imagine I've wasted my time," she said with indifference.

"You're one of the family, my dear," Galen said, with marked kindness : "It has its drawbacks."

She looked at him gratefully. "And its happy moments," she said frankly, warmly. "You're very good, Paul."

At once, she saw in his face that he was going to ask to be paid for his kindness. She felt a familiar chill. What is it ? she wondered scornfully. Before she could expect what was coming, it came — and it horrified her.

In his kind voice Galen said, "Well, my dear Marie, you can do something for me. The French colonel has just arrived : he may be more amiable than his adjutant : in any case, you know how to talk to them better than I do—" he saw the change on her face and went on with an even smoother calm — "they're sensible enough but abominably touchy. . . . I want you to go across and try to see the colonel himself about Heinrich. Will you ? "

Her feeling of revulsion was so strong that she could not at once control herself, could not, as she sometimes did, call up an image of her husband to help her against his family. She made a confused gesture. "I can't. It's impossible. It's quite impossible." In a lower voice — because she was ashamed to say it to them — she added, "I'm the very last person you should send."

Lotte said fiercely, "I wouldn't ask them for anything, the brutes. Why should we give them the chance of a good laugh ? "

"You mustn't go near them, of course," her mother said. "But there is no reason why Marie shouldn't, she's French."

"Do you think that makes it easier ? " Marie said.

"More suitable," Bertha von Leyde answered in her driest voice.

42

So I have not advanced an inch since I came ? Marie thought. Her body seemed to have become as clumsy as Anna's, but she made an effort : one of her light movements — it lifted an immense weight — brought her to her mother-in-law's chair. " I'm not French," she said, smiling. " I changed when I married — my habits and feelings as well as my country. Why, I've even made myself like red cabbage — I used to detest it. . . . I can't change myself back at a moment's notice. I'm von Leyde now, I'm German. I'm absolutely German."

" My good girl," Bertha said coldly, " I don't disbelieve you for a moment. But Heinrich is my grandson and he's in danger while you stand here blathering." The last word had all the effect, in her harsh voice, of an insult.

" They certainly don't think she's French," Lotte said.

Galen's voice brushed aside this female chatter : amiable as always, it had caught up a thread of severity all the more noticeable that he seemed to be pleading with her.

" Marie, my child, you feel just what I should feel in your place. But put yourself in mine, in Anna's. If I thought they would let me beg them to release the boy, I'd go at once. But you saw for yourself, the mere fact that I was an officer is against me, they intend to humiliate us — it's natural — I expected it, and I must admit that it's perfectly natural."

Bertha von Leyde leaned forward : she had passed into the self-pitying stage of one of her emotional scenes. " I never thought you would think only of yourself," she groaned. " Poor Johann. Sometimes I feel almost thankful he's dead, and out of this."

All this time Anna was silent, standing, her thin body awkwardly thrust forward, a little apart from them all. She scarcely seemed to be listening, and she looked away when Marie looked at her.

Marie knew that she was being driven. She turned again to Galen. " You're making a mistake, Paul," she said firmly. " Pleading with them only hardens the French : they look on it as a form of cheating and resent it. I know that. . . . And you're wrong if you think they're susceptible. They're not. They respect women more than—" she hesitated — " than we do. They think of women as equals — different but equal. . . ." She smiled. " It's ridiculous, of course."

Galen spoke to her with a coldness she had never had from him — he had always been polite and gentle, a friend.

" I don't understand you, Marie. Are you a coward ? "

" No more of a coward than your wife."

" Leave Anna alone," he said severely. " You have nothing to do with her. What do you mean ? "

" That Anna is not a coward. But she hasn't said anything."

They looked at Anna, all of them. She looked back at Marie without a change in the simple submissiveness of her face, without even reproach. She said nothing. She had covered herself with a silence on which nothing took. Marie had the sensation of climbing this silence — climbing and slipping.

" Have you lost your tongue, girl ? " Bertha said angrily. " Why don't you speak ? Anyone would think you don't care what happens to your son."

" Of course she cares," Lotte said warmly. " Poor Anna."

Anna made an effort to obey her mother. " I was thinking . . ." her voice dragged, and then quickened slightly . . . " when I spoke to the French soldier, and begged him to take me too — he looked at me, right in my face, and said : Don't be silly, if it was you you wouldn't

vant your mother to be arrested as well, now would you ?
. . He was very young — and thin. He had blue eyes.
Ie seemed shocked because I expected him to arrest
ne."

Her mother crimsoned with impatience. " Is that all
ou can say ? "

" I'll go," Marie said. " I'll try what I can do."

" There, I knew you would do the right thing," Bertha
cried. " You're not quite heartless."

" Thanks, Marie," Galen said. He was moved. " I
hink you'll find I was right," he added, smiling. " The
French — I learned a great deal about them in four years
— the French can persuade themselves of anything, any
nonsense that bolsters up their idea of themselves as uniquely
civilised. I can't flatter them, I'm too blunt and simple.
But you'll know just what to say."

" You're right," Lotte said drily. " She'll get on better
vith her friends when she's alone with them."

" Lotte, you shock me," Galen said. " Why do you
persist in treating your sister-in-law as though she were an
enemy ? She's behaving with courage and intelligence. It
ouches me very much. You're ungenerous."

He walked with dignity to open the large door leading
o the other wing. Marie followed him, slowly. She was
n despair — but she had taught herself to despair with a
ight step, and with that movement of her body a dancer
makes in the instant of floating off. As she passed her,
Anna said in a low voice,

" Oh, Marie, I would go myself if it was any use."

" I wouldn't," Lotte said loudly.

Paul von Galen turned his head to say gently, " Marie
s showing herself a better German than you, my child."

That is precisely true, Marie thought bitterly. Nothing
ould be more like us than this clumsy intrigue. She felt

grieved and ashamed. She looked round at them with a
smile, and went out quickly.

3

She was halted at the top of the stairs by the sentry.
He left her to wait on the landing while he went in with
her request. Through the heavy door she could hear the
voices but not what was said. She could not, in spite of
her anger, stop trembling. To steady herself, she repeated
You are a German, you are going into a French room, you
are going to enter France, an enemy country. The soldier
opened the door again, beckoned her, and held it open.
She saw that France is an almost empty room, with naked
windows. All the Gothic trappings had been stripped off
and wooden tables and chairs imported. I had no idea
there was so much light in this room, she thought. . .
The English captain — she had forgotten him — was standing when she came in ; Major Aubrac, seated at one of the
tables, glanced at her but did not move.

" It is kind of you to see me," she said to him in French.

" Speak German, please. What is it you want ? "

She looked round her for a chair. Captain Long pushed
one forward : she smiled at him — this is a lesson in deport-
ment, she thought — and seated herself. " You have
arrested my young brother-in-law," she said in a precise
voice, " Heinrich. . . . I came to tell you what happened."

Aubrac answered her with a biting civility. " Is that
all ? I've already been told what happened. You're wasting
my time, Frau von Leyde."

France, she said to herself, is a politeness which turns
to ice in your hand. She looked at hers, then lifted her
head to look at Aubrac.

" Were you told that he lost his head when he saw you

men carrying off a cupboard his mother values — and you had promised it to her ? "

" You are mistaken. I had given an order for the thing to be taken to Frau von Galen, the men were carrying it round outside. That's all."

" Oh, then — since it was a mistake . . ." she said joyfully. She was conscious — as a man fishing, intent only on his line, might notice that there are trees on one side of him, that they have leaves — of the young English officer watching her : he had been watching her since she came in, without curiosity, with an almost impersonal kindness. He is hardly an enemy, she thought, and ignored him.

" His mistake," Aubrac said, " was that he struck one of the men — a corporal."

" I know. And I know that corporals are the most sensitive points in any army . . . and capable of becoming heaven knows what. But surely—" she lifted her hands — " the majesty of the French army isn't in danger from a boy of twelve ? "

" What a pity all Germans are not of your way of thinking," he said calmly. " My cousin was a schoolboy of twelve three years ago when he was put against a wall in our village, and shot."

Marie felt cold : it was a real cold, it came from yet another France — where children are killed. I ought to have known, she thought, with horror. It wasn't in Normandy . . . but what do I know even about Normandy, living there as I did, and leaving when I did ? She stared at Aubrac for a moment, and said in a low voice,

" Forgive me — I should have spoken more carefully if I'd known."

He smiled slightly. " But how could you have known that all Germans are not charming and sensitive ? Decent kindly people, only anxious to save the French from their slovenly ways. Your own experience was fortunate."

His irony gave her a chance to recover. "Yes — it wa.
— though you don't mean that," she said gravely. "Bu
why punish me for it ? And why punish a German school
boy for a crime he's innocent of ? Entirely innocent
And you won't pretend that what he did this morning is a
crime. I beg you to let him off."

"It's not in my hands," Aubrac said curtly.

"Really not ? "

"No."

She stood up, and made a step or two towards the
door, then turned on him. "Why do you speak to me in
German ? "

"I imagined you would prefer it."

"I don't."

"I prefer not to speak French to you," he said smoothly

He is implacable — but deathly tired, she thought. She
smiled. "You should at least be grateful to me for giving
you the chance to be so incorruptibly in the right."

"I'll admit one thing. You defend yourself like a
Frenchwoman. With your wits."

"If you can suggest any other method," she said lightly
She felt a faint excitement, almost pleasure. "But probably
you feel I should have left my wits in France." She hesi
tated, then half closed her eyes and jumped. "With all
the other things I left there. My childhood. All my book
and my bicycle."

He looked at her. "Some child will find them," he said
meditatively. "There still are children in France, I believe.'

She had forgotten that she must interest him and defend
herself : she let go, opening her hands.

"I'm not absolutely sure that I'm not one of them
Sometimes I dream that I'm going to wake up and hear
a pigeon, one of ours, and I shall jump out of bed and see

it walk across the yard. . . ." This morning, she thought, it was this morning. " And downstairs, my mother — my young mother, you know, rather impatient, but not old or tired — is hurrying because it's a fine day, and we shall go out together . . . and then . . ." She felt an immense regret — but for what ?

Aubrac was silent.

It was after all something that her mind — how was it that she had not noticed the deafness in this house, the absence, when she spoke, of an echo ? — felt the pressure on it of another. " Then the clocks strike, three of them — exactly on the hour and all together." She smiled. " That only happens here."

" It could only happen here," Aubrac said. " To the most drearily efficient people on earth. And the most anxious."

" Yes, aren't we ? " she said. She moved her hands easily and lightly. " And if you know that about us, surely — even though you hate us — for what we did — for your young cousin — surely you must have felt sometimes, or only once, that a German is a human being ? And even if at the same moment you only wanted to get rid of him by killing him, you must have stopped hating him — for a moment. One can hate an enemy, but not mere human beings, so silly as they are."

She had made a mistake. She could not imagine what she had done, but her hold on him, imperceptible as it had been, was finished.

" Yes. You're only too right. I did once look closely at another — what did you say ? — mere human being. I was tied to a chair at the time, and the German was doing something to me so unpleasant and unmentionable that I won't mention it. I was hating him. His eyes were rather near mine, and I stared at them, into them, and hated him.

Suddenly — I wasn't expecting it — he stared back : I saw the pupils of his eyes, and behind them I saw the simple dull creature he was, a husband or a father, a clerk perhaps, or a gardener ; I felt sorry for him, for his dullness — poor devil, he didn't even know what a good onion soup ought to taste like, or how simple it is to do nothing for a whole day : and at the same moment I knew he had seen me, myself, Michel Aubrac, thirty-three years old, born in a village near Bordeaux, and living poorly but very happily thank you in Paris — until August 1939. It was distinctly odd — even exciting — as if I were flying — oh, extraordinary. Then I felt grief, yes, grief. . . ." He had been speaking with a light bitterness, almost smiling. His voice changed and became coldly correct. " That spoiled it, I was back in my chair — with my German. . . ."

The young woman was scarcely able to speak. She shivered. Forcing herself to look at this last, terrible, France, she turned — without meaning it — to the third person in the room, the neutral. He was not now, if he ever had been, on her side : standing a little way behind him, he was watching Aubrac.

" Yes — and then ? " she said inaudibly.

" We both went on, where we had left off for a moment," Aubrac said coolly.

" You make me ashamed."

" Of being a German ? "

" No, of not being able to bear unhappiness," she said in the same low steady voice. " If all that had happened to me — so that I hated my life — I should kill myself. . . ." She smiled. " As quietly as possible, of course."

" Really ? How absurd. I was only proving to you that men can hate each other — even as poor simple naked human beings."

" All Germans are not brutes," she said. " My husband

— he was a soldier — was good, kind, brave."

" And an invader of your country."

" He was like you — under orders."

" You tell yourself that, do you ? " he said quietly, with a bitter contempt. " I had not had orders to cross the frontier into another country, and to kill and torture people whose crime was that they disliked war." He shook with his cold anger. " When this good kind brave young man reached Normandy, and you kissed his hands, it was, was it ? because you knew there was no French blood on them."

The tension in his body made him seem taller. She felt a confused anger move in her in answer : it was fully as cruel as his, and as ironical and unforgiving — if she were in the wrong, that only was the difference between them, there was no other.

" Why should there be ? No one had tried to stop him."

Captain Long took a sudden step forward. He had the sense that he was moving into an electrified field between these two — enemies, were they ? He had no idea. His affection for Aubrac did not throw any light for him on the older man's nature : he saw, as anyone might have seen, that Aubrac was bitter, disliking even himself, but he pretended that the real thing in him was his ironical gaiety — knowing very well that the real thing was a wound, to his humanity, which put Aubrac completely out of reach, there was no way in which he could be helped. Knowing this, he rested his hands on the table and looked at him with an air of amused anxiety. Aubrac gave him an impatient glance.

" What ? What did you say ? " he asked in a sharp voice.

" Nothing. What I was going to say was : Why not let me speak to the colonel about young Leyde ? There doesn't seem much point in holding him. He's a young ass and he's made a fool of himself, that's all — we shall only start up a lot of bad feeling if we punish him. It's not worth it."

He had spoken slowly and lazily — to give Aubrac no excuse for thinking about him that he was not just a simple-minded young Englishman. He took care not to show his relief when Aubrac laughed at him.

" You mean that it would be a pity to spoil our honeymoon with the Boches! Not worth it! Do you know, you're quite unbearable. That's what no one can bear — the way an Englishman lounges about the world mumbling, It's not worth it — and slipping things into his pocket."

" You can look in mine."

With a more nearly friendly malice, Aubrac said, " I'm to send you to the colonel to ask him to forgive this poor little Boche ? "

" I shall say you approve," Long said.

" Thanks," Aubrac said. " I'll go myself. I don't trust you."

He pulled himself up and limped out of the room, without glancing at Marie. There was a moment's silence, and she felt the air in the room become light, she could breathe. Long said formally,

" Won't you sit down again ? "

She would have no use, in talking to this young man, of anything except her politeness, and her gaiety. " I managed badly . . . if Heinrich is let off, he'll owe it to you — you are very kind." She almost yawned.

" I'm afraid I wasn't thinking of the boy," Long said gently. He hesitated. " I was thinking of Aubrac — it's bad for him to get worked up. He ought to have a very quiet life."

She was vexed with herself. Her feeling of boredom — when she thought he had come to her help because he admired her — was a vulgar mistake, of hers. She said ironically,

" Was that why he came here ? "

" He came because he knew it would be unpleasant,"
Long said in his low, rather abrupt voice. " He thinks
it's time that young Frenchmen stopped hating — and this
is no country to come to if you want to forget what you
know about cruelty and hatred. The next criminal we
catch may not be innocent. I don't feel that this country is
repentant or very friendly. Even this village. . . . A murder
or two, a few French and English soldiers ambushed and killed
— and we shall become unpleasant. Brutality is catching."

" You've nothing to fear in this village," she told him
drily. " My brother-in-law — Colonel von Galen — is the
one man everyone, whatever his politics, respects. And he
is determined to have peace."

There was a silence. She reflected that she would have
known he was English, simply by his ability to say nothing :
Englishmen feel no obligation to be entertaining. . . . She
was attending so carefully to his silence that his next remark
startled her.

" They're kind to you, are they ? "

" Who ? "

" Your in-laws. . . . I beg your pardon. I had no right
to ask that question."

" Why not ? " she said, smiling. " You ought to know
what sort of people you're dealing with. This is their
family house, they used to grow wine, they were modestly
rich, they read — they used to read French, they travelled,
they adore cactus plants, Wagner, and strong black coffee
with cream, they cry when they fall in love, they have a
swarm of cousins, and the younger ones, even the plainest,
can't enjoy a fine day without taking off all their clothes,
they are possessive, sentimental, nervous — in short, German.
. . . None of this is true about Anna von Galen, who is a
saint."

" I'm sure they're very pleasant."

" Pleasant Boches ! What nonsense," she mocked him.

" I've known several. They're easy to get on with. Easier than the French."

" You haven't lived in a German family, you have no idea how little malice there is in their unkindness. They're at the mercy of their feelings, you know — and very greedy."

" How long have you been here ? "

" I came last year, in April."

Again he said nothing, watching her. She did not resent questions in which — she felt it — there was no curiosity except precisely that pure inquisitiveness of the English, which has rewarded them with an empire. " Is this an examination ? " she said lightly.

" Of course not."

She smiled at him. " That was very stupid of me."

" I was indiscreet, I apologise."

She felt an impulse to talk to him frankly. " My husband knew the English would invade . . . we had been married two years . . . he thought he had better bring me here before it was too late. . . . You know, when he came to France, the war was over — he came from Russia — he hadn't killed any Frenchmen." With a return of mistrust and pride she added haughtily, " Please don't repeat this."

After a moment Long said, " Are you happy ? "

She made a gesture of indifference, almost disdain. " This is my home, my sisters- and brothers-in-law are my brothers and sisters. I've become a German."

" That can't be easy."

" Don't imagine that I feel it was a fatal mistake," she cried lightly, " or a treachery, or a —a moral error, to marry a German."

What made her deny what she had never believed ? Surprised, vexed, she was going to add something severe nd snubbing. The door behind her opened, Major Aubrac ame into the room, seated himself at his table, and spoke vithout looking at her.

" The colonel has sent for Colonel von Galen. You can o."

To reach the door on to the landing, she had to pass im ; he did not look up until Long, closing the door after er, came back to the centre of the room. Then he said milingly, " And what have you been saying ? Were you naking love to her ? Don't."

" Good God, no," Long answered calmly.

" You do it without noticing," Aubrac said, " you're so nnocent — I suppose it's innocence. You pick up hand-erchiefs and open doors for a woman as if you were just ble not to kiss her, you're gentleness itself — and it means xactly nothing. And you're surprised and shocked when vomen who are not so unfeeling as Englishwomen fall in ove with you. You're a nuisance — except as a soldier."

Long smiled at him. " Kind of you."

Aubrac rested his arms on the table and leaned back. You do me good, Adrian. But you make me feel old, old. . . And uncertain," he added softly, " I know too much nd it's all nonsense."

I'm a war ahead of you, he reflected. Born in 1910, he retended that he could remember those few moments when fe had the taste of security, that is, of a good second-rate vine, rolls, country butter, middle-class comfort, a little ulgar, no doubt, but modest and sensitive — a single act f injustice, a civilian harshly treated by an officer, set it uzzing like a swarm of bees. In fact, he had two memories f those years : one of his young mother — so that he was ever able to rid himself of the idea that grey hair and lined aces are a post-war habit of women : the other of an after-oon in summer, warm, endless — no doubt it came to an

end in August 1914, but, until then, what a climate ! . .
You can't even imagine it, he told Adrian ; it amused him
to believe that, born in 1919, Adrian had never eaten butter
unadulterated by science, one week delicious and the next
flavoured with turnip, according to the season — there are
not now any seasons. And even during the last five years
they had fought different wars. It had been the same war
— with the slight difference it makes that you are or are
not fighting in your own country, along roads which are or
are not the continuation outside you of your nerves — until
Dunkirk. After that, no likeness, not a trace. At no
moment had the Englishman to expect the treachery of a
countryman, or torture ; he knew all about danger, dis-
comfort, wounds, he knew nothing about cruelty . .
nothing, nothing, nothing. It was remarkable how little
he knew, in how few ways he was the child of his time.
In his confident happy moments, Aubrac told himself that
this ignorance of the English will save the rest of the con-
tinent, broken by its knowledge of good and evil : in others
— they came oftener — that it will ruin everything. . .
He was fond of Long.

The door opened briskly, and Colonel Maulnier came in.
He went directly to one of the long mirrors. Of medium
height, thin, sharp-featured, he had the face of a monk or
of an over-trained athlete. He was forty-eight, and he had
had trouble with a lung, but he carried himself like a
subaltern — if you believed him, his only vanity. He was
narrowly and rigidly pious ; he believed that God has the
same passion for discipline and order as a good staff officer
this allowed him to treat an irregularity as a sin, and despise
an immoral person as much as if he were a coward or lazy.
He was, but he concealed it — since this really is a sin, and
moreover frowned upon by superior officers and politicians
— cruelly ambitious.

Turning from the glass, and smiling — he had a neat humorous smile — he said,

" Where is the fellow ? Good — you've got rid of the woman : she'd better keep out of my sight, I can't stand disorderly women."

At this moment the sentry jerked open the other door. Maulnier glanced up, and his adjutant, who was looking at him, saw his face change very slightly — a gleam of recognition followed by annoyance, both formal. Paul von Galen came forward with the politeness of a host ; he bowed slightly, and received a stiff salute in return.

" I didn't expect to see you again here," he said, smiling.

" It's you, is it ? " the Frenchman said drily. " I thought I knew the name."

" If I had been told who was coming, I should have moved out with a better heart."

Maulnier became even stiffer. " It was hardly likely you would be told." He seated himself, but did not ask the German or his two officers to sit.

The air of friendly welcome did not leave Galen's face. " Oh, of course not. I hope you have everything you want ? I'm afraid the house has been rather neglected — no servants."

Maulnier cut him brutally short. " Keep to the point. The boy who has been giving trouble is your son ? "

" Yes," Galen said, with the urbanity of a man of the world, " I must apologise for his foolish behaviour. I can assure you it won't happen again."

" It certainly will not. . . . Now, sir, I haven't much time. If you're going to tell me that your son isn't right in his head, I'll hand him back to you to be kept under proper supervision. I can't have mental cases wandering about loose here. . . . Make anything you have to say very brief, please."

The German hesitated. " Colonel Maulnier," he said at last, " when I met you, a year ago, I had been doing my best to kill you — and you treated me politely and with great consideration."

" Yes, well ? " Maulnier said drily.

" Surely," Galen said in a gentle voice, " two old soldiers like ourselves should be able to talk to each other, as soldiers ? "

It was now Maulnier who hesitated. He drummed on the table, then, almost unnoticeably, relaxed. " To tell you the truth, I didn't expect you to survive."

" Ah, I see," the German said, with a smile. " You were speaking to the dying man, not to the German soldier. . . . Yet what had I done except obey my orders ? Reasonable orders. You, as a French officer, know that I fought normally and decently."

Behind the backs of both colonels, Aubrac looked at Long with a comically resigned face. . . . Now that the old man has been tricked into an argument, we're here for ever. . . . Maulnier delighted in an audience, even of journalists . . . even, it seemed, of one lanky Boche. . . . " Of course I do," he was saying briskly. " I'm not a journalist."

" Then why treat me now, in my own house," Galen said gently, " as if I were a criminal ? War is always war. Between soldiers."

Maulnier's face had assumed the alert humorous expression it put on for press photographers.

" War happens to be my career. I have nothing against it, it makes life all the more worth living — but I have everything against the Germans, you've invaded us three times in a lifetime, ruined our country, and deported or murdered more than a million young Frenchmen. Not to speak of French women. That's not war."

Aubrac could bear it no longer. " I beg your pardon, sir," he said softly, " but surely that's just what it is ? German war."

Galen turned on him the friendly smile which made his narrow face with its sunken cheeks and long nose so curiously pleasant. " Ah, I've heard others of your countrymen say that," he said genially. " I still read your reviews, and any of your new books I can get hold of, I always did ; as an amateur I admire French writers — just as I admire and, as a soldier, respect your courage. It defeated us," he finished, smiling.

" Good of you," Aubrac said. " I'm sorry I don't play. I've never felt much respect for your army or its victories."

He was disappointed to see that Galen did not change colour and was so little moved by this insult that he still smiled.

" You're too severe," he murmured.

" You owed them both, it seems to me," Aubrac said in a calm voice, " to a good deal of coldly induced brutality — as well as to a rather longer process of foul diplomacy. You wanted to conquer Europe, and so you became what you are. You may think it was worth it."

The German looked at him. " Some things have to be done — to save the life of a nation — things I shouldn't do for myself. You can understand that. As a good Frenchman — desperately anxious to save France from going to pieces — you wouldn't be afraid to be harsh. Even cruel."

Aubrac rested both hands on the back of a chair. It held him up — he was tired of standing, his body ached — and allowed him to grip it as though he were strangling the other man. His bitterness and his contempt fought in him with his sense that the Germans are an absurd people — simply that, absurd. The delight with which they turn their bodies into automata, their persistence in the most cruel of all religions, the pleasure with which they inflict pain, on each other as well as on deliberately sought-out enemies — all absurd. To strengthen the tribe, they will use anything, any cruelty, any treacherous lie ; they call it devotion to Germany, and ask : But don't you care as much for France ? . . . There was an answer, but he could not give it to this cultivated intelligent ape. . . . *No !* No, because France must be human as well as strong ; the French tribe — with its ten-year-old straw hats worn only for fishing, its hundred-year-old mattresses faithfully remade a hundred times, and its recipe for cooking an eel, invented in 1446 by the ancestor who also added a corner of a field to the property — while it was learning to increase and multiply must also learn the secrets of justice and the humanities. . . . But say that to this bony rationalist, this amateur of Montaigne and the thumb-screw !

" You've said it. I should be afraid."

Galen smiled.

" I should be afraid," Aubrac repeated, " to teach Frenchmen that it's only weak to be content with what you have—" of course, if you can take in the other corner of the field, all the better — " and to enjoy your life. They might become useless as human beings. . . ." He added, with a gross contempt, " But you don't understand what I mean, of course."

Galen winced — in spite of himself : but he said coolly, " Perhaps I don't. But I do begin to see what had happened to France, and why we defeated you so easily. . . . Until the Russians and Americans came to your help and defeated us."

Maulnier had listened to this interruption with displeasure : he cut it short by saying in a grave precise voice,

" Let me tell you that if no one had helped us — if you had crushed France — God would have seen to it that we lived on as a memory. Without France, who would know what a human country is ? Tell me that."

" Much good that would have done you," Galen said gently. " We Germans fight differently for our country."

" The world knows how you fight," Aubrac said with distaste.

" We taught it something," the German snapped. He controlled himself at once. Turning to the silent Long, he said smiling, " I'm sure you agree with me that now the only problem is — as your great poet said — to *Pluck from the memory a rooted sorrow*, and plant the future."

" We're doing our best," Long said drily.

Colonel Maulnier stood up — a gesture of dismissal. ' I'll release the boy. But make sure it doesn't happen again. Do you understand ? "

" I'm very much obliged to you." Galen moved towards the door, his head bent, then turned and added quietly, " I should like you to realise that I understand, and accept fully, the logic of defeat, I want to do everything I can to prevent trouble in this district — I want to prepare for peace."

Maulnier turned his back. " I shall see that there is no trouble."

" Forgive me," Galen said in a friendly voice. " I have no right to offer you a loyal . . . pact."

" No chance of loyalty exists between men and wolves," the Frenchman said. " It's neither suitable nor permissible."

" I expect you are right."

The German withdrew with a polite ease, like a man leaving his guests to themselves for a moment.

" Ridiculous fellow," Aubrac said, as the door closed. " Vain as a woman. I can't stand him."

Maulnier was moving towards the other door : he had taken for himself, since austerity was a part of his creed, the bare room which had been a gun-room. " You're unjust to him, as a matter of fact," he said in his neat sharp voice.

" He's extremely brave. I came across him in Normandy
when I was attached to an American division. They had
been shelling a fort for three or four days, giving it everything they had ; we were still being fired at, mortars and
machine-guns, on the fourth day, when we took it — and
found one survivor — this fellow. What's more, he'd been
the only survivor for forty-eight hours. He collapsed at
once — very severe wounds and hunger. We exchanged him
later — and I heard he'd been sent home. He must be
pretty well crocked. . . . Well, I hope that's the end of him.'

And he went out, so sharply that Long had to jump to
open the door.

Aubrac looked after him with an ironical smile. " He
enjoyed himself."

" Who ? "

" I mean the old man. He loves to put on an act, and he
gets so few chances. . . . What no one realises — except
me — is that he's sincere, absolutely sincere. All this piety
and asceticism, and the happy warrior, it's the real man — he
is pious, he is the happy warrior, he has only to be himself to
be a magnificent actor, the very model of a general. . . ."

" If anyone was acting just now," Long said slowly, " it
was surely von Galen."

" What, the Boche ? Oh, nonsense, my dear fellow.
Nonsense ! "

Chapter Three

I

AFTER three months the house settled into an uneven
balance — in the main wing the French had set going a

routine of life which differed hardly at all from the one they
would have lived in no matter what small garrison town at
home, and they put up more or less cheerfully with a score
of inconveniences, the result of refusing to change one, even
the newest, of their habits : in the other, Bertha von Leyde
complained ceaselessly that she could not breathe, there was
no room ; the window in her bedroom faced south and the
shutters were broken, so that she was forced to gasp in the
heat ; to make up for what she had lost, in comfort and a
raddled splendour, she added every day another grievance
to the scale ; it sank as the other wing, lightened of its false
Gothic, rose like a bubble from the untrimmed lawn. It
was unjust.

The weight of their mother's temper was borne, as always,
by Anna. Happily preparing her marriage and plundering
her mother's and sister's wardrobe for dresses to cut up and
remake, furnishing, with what she could pick up, the two
rooms she had managed to get in the village, Lotte escaped.
. . . This afternoon, as soon as she was alone in the kitchen,
after Anna had set the table with the coffee cups, and gone
out, she began searching the cupboards. She heard Richard's
steps in the stone-flagged passage, and ran to meet him.
Normally a little muted in its prettiness, even a little hard,
her face became all at once joyous and alive. She flung her
arms round him, and butted him gently with her head —
she was ashamed of her tenderness, that was why she made
so many of the movements of a rough little animal.
" Richard ! "

" Lotte ! "

Lotte twitched his jacket — it fitted him at a few points ;
when she had adjusted these she had done her best for him.

" I've just come in. I've been scrubbing the floor in
our room," she said boisterously. " And what do you think
I found this morning, at the back of Langer's shop ? A

casserole ! Yes, really. Now we have a perfect kitchen shelf — casserole, frying-pan, kettle, and a little pan for boiling an egg. You know, you must never use an egg-pan for anything else — or you'll get warts."

" What nonsense," Richard muttered. He blinked a little, as though he were dazzled — as he was.

" It's true, my little dog, really true."

" Oh, Lotte," he said despairingly, " you won't like living in two rooms behind a shop — and such poor little rooms."

She laughed at him. " Don't talk rubbish — dog. I'm only so thankful we can't live here. If it hadn't been for those beasts taking the house, we should have found ourselves living with the family. What an escape ! "

" If only I had more money."

" Mother is going to give me her best linen, every sheet. And tomorrow I'm going to make our bed up," Lotte said simply. " She really promised it to Anna, but who cares ? I shall laugh when I see Anna's face — all her sheets have been darned until it's like sleeping on nettles."

She laughed loudly, but Richard frowned. His pride — of a respectable hard-working family — was touched. " We ought not to take it," he said gravely. " I don't like your mother giving us so much. She's too generous."

" Nonsense," Lotte cried, " she likes it. She's silly enough to give me anything I ask for, and if Anna says a word she'll tell her to shut up. But Anna won't, she knows better."

" Even Anna thinks you're rash to marry a poor man," he said gloomily.

She tried to shake him, seizing him by his shoulders. " Who's poor ? " she said roughly. " I call a man poor if he's lazy or useless or a coward. You're never lazy, and you know how to put up shelves and make a garden — your mother told me — and you have your three medals and both your arms and legs. I shouldn't love you without them."

" Oh, my little love, I depend on you so much. . . ."

" And as soon as we have a son you'll teach him to swim and climb trees, and run — and you'll make me a chair for him. We don't need money ! "

Richard turned away, freeing himself. " A son ? " he said, quietly bitter — " what use is it having a son ? He hasn't a future."

" There's always a future for a strong clever child," Lotte said gently. Suddenly she was a woman not a hoyden. " Yours will be strong and clever. Don't be silly, my darling. What have we to be afraid of ? "

" Everything ! " he said, with quick uncouth passion.

" Richard ! What do you mean ? "

" I'd like to leave this country—" words sprang from him, thickly and suddenly — " I hate all this cruelty and these poor silly old magistrates and school teachers shot at their desks for treachery, and the continual spying and the hatred. I'd give anything to take you to some place where a postman is a postman and not a murderer or a man living in terror of being murdered."

She looked at him almost timidly. " Where could we go ? "

" We might get to South America. . . . If people hate each other there, at least it isn't their duty. . . . Oh, Lotte, if we could only get away——"

He seized her, and held her as though he were saving her. She freed her arms to touch him, stroking his face gently, soothing him — " There are two of us. We shall be safe together — in our two rooms. We'll hide there, my little dog, we'll hide ourselves."

" Oh, my love, my dear," he muttered.

She pushed him away. "Ssh, I hear mother. . . She's coming to see what sort of cakes Anna has made and choose the largest one for herself."

Bertha von Leyde's face, so heavy in repose, morose and bored, became soft and foolish when she saw her Benjamin.

"Well, Richard, my dear ? . . . Ah, Lotte, what have you been doing all day ? "

"Looking for dinner plates," the girl said, in a voice of deepest dejection. "I can't find any anywhere."

"You can have my Sèvres," Bertha said fondly. "It's all here — except the lid of one tureen that clumsy fool Anna dropped and it broke . . . the fool ! "

Lotte went through a movement of surprised delight "Oh, thank you. Do you hear that, Richard ? "

"I heard you ask for it," he said, unsmiling.

"What nonsense," Bertha exclaimed, "she didn't ask. I meant it for you both."

Lotte spoke in Richard's ear. "Idiot . . . don't spoil everything with your foolishness."

Bertha had walked to the table and was bending greedily over a plate of small cakes : after a time she moved it nearer to her own place. "Where is Anna with the coffee ? I'm hungry."

"Changing her dress, of course, so that Paul won't put her through an inspection," Lotte said contemptuously. She did not notice that the door had opened behind her. "I can't imagine why she gives in to his fussiness. It's bad enough that she has to work like a slave, without spoiling a selfish husband. She's soft."

Followed by his wife, Paul von Galen came into the room. Lotte swung round. He looked at her with his pleasant candid smile — "There's only one way to live in a kitchen, Lotte. And that's to fuss, as you call it, about the decencies. Anna has to cook — that's no reason why she should dress like one."

Taken aback, the girl said defiantly, " She exhausts herself to please you. One of these days she'll die, and it will be your fault."

Anna had seated herself at the table, behind the coffeepot : she looked up with her grotesque gentle smile. " There are so many ways of dying. If you know which of them is going to be mine, Lotte, don't tell me."

Eyeing the plate with the coquetry of a spoiled child, Bertha von Leyde said, " Now — which is the largest cake ? "

Anna took up the plate, turned it, and handed it gently to her mother. " This one."

" Ah," Bertha said, smiling.

Richard Gauss had gone clumsily to stand beside Anna, waiting until she had filled the cups, to carry them round : without noticing him, she began pushing them absently down the table : he was at a loss and stood there awkwardly. Galen beckoned, and the young man hurried to him.

" Did you get me the information I want ? " he asked in his mild voice.

" Yes, I did, sir," Richard said. He took a paper out of his pocket and passed it to Galen. " The train arrives at Mainz at twelve midnight and it passes the level crossing at ten to eleven."

" What a reliable husband you've chosen," Galen said to Lotte kindly. " You must try not to spoil him."

Lotte was embarrassed by open praise of the young man ; to hide her pleasure and embarrassment she said loudly, " The mad creature wants us to go to South America."

Galen's expression changed. " What ? What's this ? "

" I was only saying," Richard stammered — " suggesting—" he glanced at Lotte, and was filled with a reckless courage — " After all, why shouldn't we ? There's nothing to keep us here. I should like to know what peace is like. We've nothing to look forward to. No future."

Even though her hand was half-way to the plate, in the attempt to whisk off it, unnoticed, the last cake — properly speaking, Anna's, but Anna always left it for her — Bertha let it fall. She was horrified. " I couldn't let you take her to live with savages, Richard."

Galen ignored this interruption. " The future of a pair of young cowards doesn't interest me," he said harshly.

" You've no right to say that to Richard." Lotte was trembling and scarlet-cheeked with anger.

Her brother-in-law looked at her severely. " Have you encouraged him to run away ? "

" I don't know what you mean. Richard isn't a coward. But if he were it would be no business of yours, and I should marry him just the same. I should marry him if he had only one leg."

" He doesn't mean that, Lotte," the young man said softly.

" My dear fellow," Galen said in a gentler voice, " you must forgive me for being startled. No one must run away from Germany now — least of all a young intelligent man."

Richard laughed — all his awkwardness and his fear of offending, and his decent loyalty, were given away by his laugh. " I don't think I'm intelligent."

Galen redoubled his kindness. " You know how to obey."

" Yes," Richard said. " I can do what I'm told."

" And when you were in the Air Force you enjoyed obeying an order ? "

" Yes. . . . Yes, I did."

Galen leaned forward. " Do you trust me ? "

Richard spoke with an ashamed eagerness. " Of course I do, sir. Absolutely."

" Do you want to be famous ? " Galen asked, smiling.

" No ! . . . I don't want anything."

" What do you want ? "

The young man looked at Lotte. Help me, his look said. " Lotte knows."

" What does he want, Lotte ? " Galen asked kindly.

" What I want." The girl moved her hands in a gesture oddly helpless for so self-assured a young woman. " He wants us to have a house and children — and — oh, just to live." She broke off abruptly.

" My dear children," Galen said, " live, by all means. Live here, where you're needed, and don't talk childishly about running away. You don't mean it, you know, and it has an ugly disloyal sound. . . . Let's talk about something else. . . . What is this I hear about the curfew ? "

Richard withdrew, shyly and awkwardly, to the farther side of the room, and stood there, trying to believe that with his clumsily square hands and his obedience he had placed himself exactly where he could best defend Lotte from all that other humans would do to her : she joined him silently, and they stood close together, like children.

" They've put it forward," Bertha von Leyde said, " to six o'clock. How I detest the French. They're so trivial and irritating ; they remind me of your cousin Olga when I asked her about the air-raids in Berlin : she said she didn't mind the bombs so much, but she had to shelter with all her neighbours and there were fleas." A gleam of shrewd malice made her look younger. " Where is Marie ? " she asked. " I must tell her that."

" They're not all contemptible. . . . I like Maulnier. I respect him." Galen began to walk about the room : a look of sullen anger, not like him, had altered his face so that its long delicate mouth and jutting bones suggested other qualities than kindness and a passion for reason.

It was an anguish to him to feel that the French had not
enough good sense, say nothing of generosity, to see in
him a man they could talk to on equal terms. He lifted
his head sharply, and said, " The strange thing is, he has
no respect for me. . . . You understand, I don't mind it
for myself, I'm not vain. But I resent the insult to an
officer of the same rank as himself. . . . We Germans
deserve respect. It's of no importance when a politician
or a journalist lies about us — it's deplorable but it's natural.
But a man like Maulnier should know better."

" Bah, we defeated the French easily," Bertha said.

Galen smiled. " That's it, of course ! Mamma, you're
very shrewd. That explains Maulnier. . . ." His face
contracted again. " The fellow I can't stand is Aubrac.
I'm really not sane about him. It's humiliating to feel like
that. . . . He behaves quite decently, too. Better on the
whole than Maulnier."

His wife looked at him. He was irritated by this look :
there were moments, extremely rare, so rare that he knew
they were accidents, when his good clumsy Anna collected
herself and became a woman he would never have married
— and in fact he had not married her — detached, clear-
sighted, amused.

" He makes you want to kill him," she said calmly.

Forcing himself to smile at her, he said, " I can't imagine
why. I'm reasonably calm and rational."

" He laughs at you."

He controlled his anger. " Well, really, Anna——" the
moment had gone, there was no one in front of him but
a submissive woman. Smiling, he added gently, " What
nonsense you talk. . . . It's extraordinarily vexing about
the curfew. I've arranged to go and see Altdorf. I can't
possibly get back here by six. I could get a permit, perhaps,
but I must say I dislike asking for one."

Marie came into the room. She had scarcely taken three steps towards them when Lotte said maliciously,

" Get Marie to ask for you. She's so clever with the dear English and the dear French."

" It wasn't my vest that blew off the line and wrapped itself round the sentry's neck," Marie said lightly. Why, she thought sadly, do you force me to make fun of you and tell these others about an accident you thought disgraceful and humiliating ?

" I thanked him when you asked him to bring it back," Lotte stammered furiously. " He grinned like a monkey. I suppose you would have flung both arms round him."

" Lotte, Lotte," her mother said indulgently, " don't be absurd."

Paul von Galen lifted his hand, to silence them. They were silent. He was less amiable than he had been three months ago. Not more exacting — that would have been difficult — but, without ever losing his temper, he had managed to bring even Bertha von Leyde into a rather apprehensive state of mind about him : she rarely scolded him now ; she explained it to herself by saying : Paul is very nervous, it's his wounds.

" As a matter of fact, it's the English captain who is on duty this evening. I happen to know that. Maulnier and the other fellow are going, they may have gone already, into Mainz, to be there when the English members of parliament arrive. . . . I'm told they're all socialists and pacifists," he said, smiling : " they've come to see whether it's true that German children have forgotten what it's like to wear shoes, and that the younger ones can't read or write because their school books have been taken from them and no new ones provided. . . . Well . . . I hope they'll learn a little of the truth."

" At their best — in their good moments," Marie said

calmly, " the English have a sense of responsibility."

" They're better than the French," Bertha retorted.
" No — worse. Stupider and much stronger."

" Is that what the English officer talks to you about ? "
Lotte said to Marie, in her loudest voice.

" I should be very grateful, Marie, if you would in fact
speak to Captain Long," Galen said pleasantly. " Tell him
I should like a permit to be out tonight. . . . I've noticed
that you occasionally come across him in the grounds, and
talk to him — it seemed to me, amiably."

This despair, how familiar it was, and how light, a bubble
escaping from the heavy German bog, and how many lessons
she had still to learn, of repulsion, of withdrawal. She
could only defend herself by a directness and simplicity,
and a natural politeness, removed as far as possible from the
tortuous emotions hemming her in. She must not use
insults or cruelty, or any of the superb sentiments that would
come suitably and naturally from another woman, more
intelligent or self-conscious, in her place. . . . She had
deliberately chosen this place. . . .

" He never asks questions," she said gaily. " We've
discussed the garden once or twice. And books."

" You might tell us when you get so far as discussing
the weather," Lotte said. " That will be really exciting."

" Come now," Galen smiled, " you're already on friendly
terms with him."

" It's not difficult with the English, my dear Paul. They
ought to dislike us for having been defeated, but they don't
seem to."

Lotte made a sound that was an infant echo of her mother's
formidable laugh — you could imagine what it would be
like full-grown. " He knows you're not a German ! Thank
goodness he does."

Marie did not mind this young enmity, but Galen's

reassuring " My dear Marie, I know how very loyal you are "
was suddenly too much.

" When you think you can make use of me," she said
in a light voice, " I'm a German who only happens to have
been born French. . . . *I* am the only member of the
family who thinks of Marie von Leyde as a German all the
time."

" How ungrateful you are," her mother-in-law said
sharply. " Poor Johann."

Her husband's name coming at the end of this reproof
gave her for one moment the illusion that if she made a
direct appeal she would reach in Bertha von Leyde her
recesses of kindness and honesty. She touched the old
woman's hand, and spoke with a quiet half-desperate
seriousness — " For Johann's sake, Mamma, try to trust
me. I really am to be trusted. You're my family."

" Don't let's have a scene, Marie," the baroness said
coldly.

Marie was spared the need to smile. She smiled none
the less, but the others were not looking at her : Anna
said in a low anxious voice, " I think someone is coming."

They watched the door leading to the main wing. Someone knocked.

Richard started forward. " Shall I open it, sir ? "

With a barely noticeable hesitation, Galen said, " Yes.
Yes, of course." His expression, as Richard opened the
door, became friendly and smiling. " Ah, come in, come
in," he said warmly.

Without any marked eagerness Captain Long came in.
He saluted the baroness, and said formally,

" I beg your pardon for disturbing you, I came to say
that there's no objection to your collecting firewood in the
grounds." Turning to Anna, he added more gently, " I
came myself because I wanted to apologise to Frau von

73

Galen for the rough treatment she got this morning. I
won't happen again."

Galen swung round to look at his wife, who smiled
foolishly and helplessly, seeing her mother, too, about to
attack her, and her sister — but, no, Lotte had seized her
chance to slip out of the room ; the other door was already
closing behind her and Richard. . . . " Anna," her mother
said : " you didn't tell us you'd been insulted. You've no
excuse for putting yourself in such a position. No one
insults *me* ! "

" I didn't know I'd been insulted," Anna said simply.
" One of the soldiers told me I had no right to pick up
firewood, and he took it from me. I came home without
it. Nothing else happened." She smiled at Long without
any timidity. " You don't think I was afraid or upset ? "

" I wonder what would upset you," her mother exclaimed,
" if the coarseness and vulgarity of the French doesn't. . . ."
She stood up. " Help me to my room."

On Anna's arm, she walked stiffly and angrily from the
room — ignoring Marie, who had opened the door for them.

Galen smiled slightly, as though he were amused ; he
tried to draw Long into his unspoken comment on women's
silliness, but the Englishman stared blankly. Stretching
his smile a little, Galen said,

" May I ask you one question ? That *is* the D.S.O. you
wear, isn't it ? "

" It is, sir." Long was polite and unfriendly.

" I thought so. And a Croix de Guerre ? "

" Yes."

" You're very young to have earned so many distinctions.
I should very much like to know how it happened."

Long was silent.

" Your terrible modesty is what makes you English so
engaging," Galen said — " and so conspicuous."

Long could not help smiling. " You've seen through us, sir."

" Only as far as I see through ourselves. I've spent my life trying to cure my illusions about myself and to use fatal words like honour, prestige, sacrifice, power, calmly. Men have been getting drunk on words like these for centuries, and murdering each other in their drunken frenzy. There will be no peace on earth until a sufficient number of men are able to think soberly about them." He hesitated, and looked at the young officer with an engaging, almost an affectionate smile. " I go on saying this — in the hope that one of these days I shall be overheard by a powerful person — Mr. Churchill or Mr. Stalin."

" It might be enough," the Englishman said drily, " if you were overheard by a few of your countrymen. Try talking to the young men who murdered a whole family the other day — to punish them for reading an English newspaper."

Galen moved towards the door. " It's utterly deplorable — but what do you expect ? " he said gently. " You announced in advance that every German is a moral leper and untouchable. After the last war — in spite of everything — you were much more human."

" It was a different war."

" I see it's no use," Galen smiled. " You can't hear me."

He went out, closing the door with such care that the handle made no sound. Until it ceased turning he seemed to be in the room. Marie had watched the handle : she shrugged her shoulders lightly when she could at last feel certain he had gone, but did not move closer to the young officer. Nor did he move. The glance, of friendship, almost of complicity, he gave her would have puzzled Galen, it was direct, it showed an intimacy, but it might have

75

been a family intimacy. He took a book from the pocket of his tunic.

" Here it is. It came yesterday, from Paris." He added coolly, " I can't be in the chestnut avenue this evening, I'm on duty. I was lucky to have an excuse for coming here. . . . I'm sorry it's not a better copy."

" There can't be a better one." She held the book without opening it. " The first time I've had a French book in my hands since we left. . . . You know, I can't order one myself. I've no money, and if I had it wouldn't be worth anything in France."

" You still haven't heard from your family ? "

After a moment she said, " I didn't write to them."

" Why not ? " Long asked gently. " You're full of fears, aren't you ? "

She made a light gesture. " No, no, it's because I want to know such absurd things. I want to ask my sister if she remembered her promise — we were to think of each other for an hour every time we saw the new moon — and if she found the half-used jar of face cream I hid for her behind her books, and why isn't she reading them ? . . . How can I write such nonsense, after writing nothing for a century ? "

" You defend yourself very well," the young officer said slowly ; " you've had too much practice."

There was another brief pause. " How can I, a German, write to France ? " she said in another voice.

" You're not a German."

She had recovered herself instantly, and her gaiety. " Much you know about it ! I'm so German that I can't even enjoy bad music any longer. And I cry when I'm happy and laugh with joy when someone I like very much loses his wits or his money."

" Yes, I see. . . . And when you look at the new moon

you think in German ? For the whole hour ? "

" Don't be absurd."

" Well ? " Long said drily.

She lifted her hands again in a gesture half of despair, half mocking. " Even if it were true, what use is it ? . . . I'm sunk in Germany. Yes, sunk. There isn't even a bubble to be seen."

He leaned forward and touched the book in her hand. " There's this."

" Yes," she agreed — " a bubble. It's dangerous to send up even one. . . . I'll risk it. . . . And now you must go."

He did not move. " I'm going to ask a question. If you don't want to answer it you needn't."

Marie half closed her eyes. " Yes ? "

" I really would like to know what you think — think honestly, not defensively — of Colonel von Galen. He puzzles me."

She drew back so slightly that he did not notice it. What were you expecting ? she asked herself ironically. She spoke quickly and recklessly, to give herself no time to be cautious.

" Paul ? Oh, he's almost too sane. He's argued himself out of all his passions — except his vanity. He is terribly vain of having no vulgar passions. He's kind — and very selfish and exacting. . . . I like him very much."

" Yes, well ? "

" He uses people. It's because he thinks of himself as a great man — who ought to be spared the inconveniences of living. . . . He uses me. . . . He told me to ask you for a permit to let him go out tonight to call on one of our cousins."

Long frowned. " Tell him to ask for it himself. The old man will probably allow it, he has a weakness for him.

. . . He's an intriguer, your brother-in-law. He prefers
to go round."

" Do you think so ? I think it's because he can't bear
the sight of himself asking. He doesn't think anything
dishonest that saves his pride. . . . It's not simply pride.
. . . He believes he ought to have been the victor, he ought
always to be the victor. What has happened is unjust —
and he has to ignore it."

" Very like a Boche."

" How unfair you are," she said lightly. " You insisted
on winning, didn't you ? "

The young officer hesitated. It was rarely, so carefully
had he been brought up, in a liberal and anti-clerical house-
hold, and at the finest English school, and the right college
of the better university, for him to feel that he could speak
from his heart. And although he felt safe with this young
woman — how like an Englishman of your sort, Aubrac
would have said, to feel safe with a foreigner who is not
even innocent — he mumbled his first words, to give the
impression that he did not care whether he were understood
or not.

" Of course. . . . But we know in our bones that victory
doesn't pay — after a victory the dead will still be dead,
the war will have been a crime, and humanity will have
been poisoned. It's because we know this — and don't we
know it ! — that we begin by being defeated. We haven't
arranged for anything else ! Your dear little Germans don't
know it and they go out with a clear conscience and all the
flags flying to shout and kill and torture for victory. We
others have to drive ourselves to fight. It's not because
we're cowards, as your brother-in-law would say, but
because we're human and civilised. As soon as we see that
Germans are mad enough to want to fight to possess the
world we discover that we're willing to fight to prevent

them — that is, for justice. So we fight. And always shall."

Marie had listened to him with a light anguish. He is speaking to another young woman, she said to herself; to a young woman who might have been alive if I had not killed her. At once, she rebelled against this self-accusing and guilt — it weakened her, and it was too nearly an excuse.

She looked at him directly. "If all of them are like that, Jeannot wasn't even a German."

"Your husband?"

With a bitterness she almost succeeded in making detached, she said, "You would probably call him a good Boche."

"There are a few."

She was ashamed of her impulse to mislead him. "Perhaps — if he had lived," she said simply, "he would have changed when he came home. That would have been worse, a worse death."

The young officer was silent. After a moment he asked, "Why did you marry him?"

"I was in love. It was the first time." She felt a confused shame — as though she were giving away her husband — and relief, an unhoped-for ease and confidence. She was not really ashamed: his loyalty and good-humour made it seem right and natural, or at least not improper, not self-indulgent or indiscreet, not over-emphatic, not ill-mannered, to tell him the truth about herself. But his next question startled her.

"How did you fall in love?"

"You mean — with a German . . . a Boche?"

"If you like," he said rather drily.

Behind her air of calm and youthful irony, she gave herself up to the happiness of talking about her life to a man who — she admitted it in her heart — loved her.

" I don't know. Yes, I know. My sister — Suzanne — was fourteen when the invasion started, I was seventeen, and our father sent us both away, my mother had died that year. We live at Berthenay. Do you know it ? No, of course not, it's a small village, but it has the Loire ; it's nothing, yes, nothing, but it has the Loire — which is everything. He sent us to my grandmother in Normandy. She's very old, with old servants ; she was so afraid when she saw us that she told us we mustn't go outside the grounds of the house, and she refused to have visitors. We saw no one under seventy. We didn't mind, we could look at each other if we wanted to see someone young. We'd been there more than a year when a German general took part of the house over for his staff. One of them was a young man — it was Jeannot."

For the first time since he was killed, she saw her husband with an extreme clearness : he was looking away from her ; she felt neither self-reproach nor grief, only a friendly pity for him, so young and eager to live. . . . Without either of them noticing it, the Englishman had come closer to her. She looked at him, at his eyes, very bright, a curious greenish brown in colour, a little troubled, at his clear freckled skin and small ears. There was shrewdness as well as intelligence in his face. She half lifted her hand to touch it, and drew back. Not yet, it was not time yet. Besides, I won't move first, she thought, confused ; I may be wrong.

" I see," Long said gently.

" He was a Catholic, he spoke French. . . . It took him a long time, months, to be allowed to marry a French girl, and all the time my grandmother was writing to my father, Come and take Marie away. He didn't answer. At last she gave in and said, Very well, marry him, perhaps it is God's wish. One of the German priests married us, that

was in May 1942. . . . What was happening to you then ?
— no, don't tell me."

Long was listening to her intently. He did not take
his eyes from her face. He was frowning. " You were
much too young."

" I was nineteen," Marie said. She was shaking, an
obscure and terrible disturbance began in her, there was
something she must confess, she must forget her tricks
and tell him, this time, only the truth. Let him judge
her ; she no longer wanted to defend herself.

" I should have known — even then," she said.

" What ? "

" That we weren't free. That we were trapped."

" Is that all ? " Long said. He was still watching her,
he would only have to lift his arms and she would be held
up, saved — but he did not lift them. I am still not telling
the truth, Marie thought, trembling ; he knows that.

" No ! It was fatally wrong and ill-bred. . . . Some
differences between people can't be defied, they outrage a
sort of modesty which mustn't be outraged. . . . I admit
it now."

" You never said that until now."

They looked at each other for a moment in silence.
Marie felt a new, almost serene joy. " I shan't say it again,"
she said, smiling. " To anyone. It would be absurd for
me to pretend to be tragic."

He said softly, " Yes, quite absurd."

The air round them had been drawn tense, as though
it were a network of nerves, their own nerves — a sensation
of pure physical ecstasy. In a moment it would have been
destroyed by their falling into each other's arms ; instead
it was broken very roughly by a third person, by Heinrich
von Leyde. He came in noisily, carrying his school satchel,
and threw it on the table, then stood and glared at them,

81

his face distorted in a ridiculous fury. Long turned without haste and spoke to him with a cool but real friendliness.

" Hullo. I haven't seen you since we arrested you for assault. What have you been doing ? "

" Minding my own business," Heinrich said.

Long turned his back. " Thanks, Frau von Leyde," he said formally. He saluted her and went out. Heinrich watched him. As the door closed he ran to Marie and stood in front of her, rigid.

" What did the swine want ? "

" He came to apologise to your mother."

" To see my mother ? " the boy repeated. " Not you ? . . . I don't believe it."

" He came to see me, too. He brought something I asked him for."

" What ? " he shouted. " What are you letting the brutes give you ? "

She showed him the book. " This. This book I promised I would read to you if I could get it."

" You got it for me ? " he asked in a quieter voice ; he was still sullen.

" No, for both of us, silly boy," she said, smiling. She opened it and turned the pages. " Listen. . . . *O ma belle Angevine, ô ma douce Marie, Mon œil, mon cœur, mon sang, mon esprit, et ma vie.* . . . There you are. You see — he wrote it about me."

The change in his face was almost painful to watch ; he had become a child, nervous and over-strained, but a child, a creature with his own loyalty, joy, confidence — and his own voice which was not the echo, distorted, of adult voices.

" Don't let any of the others see it," he said. " When will you read it to me ? What does it mean ? "

" Tomorrow. I'll read to you tomorrow. We'll sneak

out together into the garden. I always believed he was writing about our village. . . . We had vines. And walnuts. And of course the Loire."

" What's so marvellous about your Loire ? " the boy asked jealously.

" I don't know. . . . I think only the light."

He hesitated. " I shouldn't mind seeing it," he mumbled.

" Some day you'll be able to go."

" Only if you come as well."

" No. I shall never go there," she said, in a light voice. " You must go alone — and come back and tell me about it. You want to be a writer — and I want you to. Very well, there's nothing better than the Loire for teaching you how to be innocent and intelligent. . . . Something to do with the light."

He swung away from her. " I've changed my mind," he said vehemently. " I shan't be a writer. Writing nowadays is a luxury, and we can't afford them, we Germans. Especially young Germans." In a voice certainly not his, he added, " Nowadays nothing counts except things like courage, blood, death."

" Good heavens," she said, mocking him gently. " What a marvellous life you're going to have."

" It's true," he insisted. " Herr Rommel says so."

" The general ? But he's dead."

" No, Herr Rommel our mathematics master."

" I hope he's as good at sums as he is about writing ! "

The boy's eyes blazed. " You wouldn't laugh if you could hear him, Marie. He knows everything about the Loire. He fought there ! He told us today that when he saw Chenonceaux he wept for joy, and he made us promise to destroy it."

" Why ? " she asked softly.

" Because the rotten French took it back from us," he stammered. " And because they call us savages. German savages."

" But you know better." She turned away from him and sat down. What can you do for a child who has been corrupted by a pride and a guilt not of his size, on whom too much has been written, too many false loyalties, too many lies ? . . . Heinrich followed her.

" Marie, do you," he said in a low voice, " think I am a savage ? "

" Germany is a great country," Marie said gently, " full of philosophers who are soldiers, and children who let a fox gnaw through their flesh."

" Then why, why do they tell lies about us ? Why don't they admire us ? "

" It's a little difficult," she said, laughing. " You change about so. One minute you're admiring Chenonceaux and weeping with joy, and the next minute you want to smash it to pieces. One minute you are my kind friendly little brother, the next you only want to punish me ! You did just now."

He looked at her with a mischievous smile. " Only when you don't do as I tell you," he chuckled. Leaning over her chair, he put his arm round her shoulders. " You don't really like Germans, do you ? "

" I married one because I liked him," she said firmly. " He was gentle and stubborn — terribly stubborn. . . . I thought I was marrying into a family of stubborn saints. . . . You can believe how I wanted to see them." She made a light gesture, lifting her hands, and letting them fall in her lap. Talking to herself, not to Heinrich — a wrong thing to do to a child — she went on, " I found distrust, dislike, loneliness, exile. I wanted to be a good German — but am I ? "

" I trust you, Marie," the boy said. " No one has ever trusted you so much as I do."

She reproached herself for forgetting — she, too — that he was twelve years old. " Thanks ! " she said, smiling.

" You don't believe me ! "

" Of course," she teased him. " And tomorrow you'll suspect me of every crime your precious Herr Rommel can multiply about me."

He bent over her again and spoke so that she could only just hear. " Marie, would you like me to prove how I trust you ? I'll tell you a deadly secret. Promise you won't tell anyone."

She was careful not to smile. " I promise."

" I knew something was going on here. But they think I'm a child and they don't tell me things. Very well, I listened. I listened behind my father's door at night, when he talks to the people he smuggles in during the day. Ah, you didn't know he did that, did you ? You see, I'm pretty clever. And what do you thing I've found out ? "

She had begun to listen to him attentively. " What ? "

He brought his mouth close to her ear. " Something's going to happen to the English swine who are coming to Mainz tonight. Something very wonderful. They're going to be shot."

She suppressed her first movement of horror, but she found that she was breathless.

" Are you sure ? "

" Absolutely sure. I don't know who's going to do it — it's a thick door, I only hear bits. I know it will happen — that's all."

Making another severe effort, she said, scarcely audibly, " But it's . . . incredible."

The boy was delighted with the effect on her of his secret. " Isn't it ? " he said happily. " No, that's wrong, it's absolutely credible. I was expecting it. They couldn't kill or deport every one of us, could they ? "

She stood up, pressing her hands together. " But why murder the first people who are coming here as friends ? Almost friends. At least they're not armed."

" Oh, I can guess why," he laughed. " It will drive into them that we can't be soft-soaped."

" Heinrich, I can't bear this," she began quietly. She struggled with a fresh access of horror. " All the misery of the world is beginning again," she said in a low voice.

Alarmed, he looked at her mistrustfully. " What do you mean ? Are you going to betray us ? " She did not answer at once. " Marie ! " he shouted.

She pulled herself together and spoke to him in her lightest voice.

" Do you think I'm mad ? It's only that I'm astonished — terribly. . . . When will it happen ? When they're getting out of the train tonight, or tomorrow morning when they go to look at the ruins ? . . ." She drew a careful breath. " I was only thinking — why choose these simple-minded liberals ? Why not an important statesman ? It would be fun to break all the rules and shoot one of the great men before the war he meant to direct has even started."

Heinrich was watching her intently. " Herr Rommel detests liberals."

" But he loves to climb a mountain before dawn," she smiled, " and come down again singing."

The boy opened his eyes widely. " How did you know ? "

" I guessed."

" He used to, but he has only one leg. . . ." He came very close to her and looked at her face. " Do you know what ? I'm sure we're going to kill all these swine, one

after another. I shall make my father trust me and let me
help."

" Why not ? " she said calmly.

" Don't you mind ? " he asked, still watching her.

She did not feel ashamed of tricking him. " I shall hate
it if you run into danger."

He began to walk about again with excitement. " What's
danger ? I should like to kill one of them with my own
hands. . . . And then kill myself."

" Why yourself ? "

The boy flung his arms out widely. " As a symbol ! "

" And then ? "

" Oh, well, I suppose nothing," he mumbled. " People
would talk about me."

" Marvellous — if only symbols had ears." She went
quickly towards him, and took him by one of his.

He was completely reassured. He trusted her again.
" Don't laugh at me," he said, twisting away from her.
" And you won't tell my father I told you about this, will
you ? "

" Of course not."

" Now read to me again."

" Not now." She was at the end of her strength.

" You must. . . . What's the matter ? Do you feel ill ?
Is something matter with you ? "

" No."

" Then you can stay and read."

He pushed her towards the table. She sat down and he
thrust the book into her hands.

" Where was I ? " I shall never reach the end of the
first line, she thought. But the cunning that came to her
help now was not hers, it was Ronsard's ; her voice as she
read became stronger and even faintly triumphant. . . .
Mon œil, mon cœur, mon sang, mon esprit, et ma vie. . . .

2

An hour later, Galen was summoned to see the French colonel. He presented himself in the sitting-room in the other wing, and found Colonel Maulnier alone; he was sitting at a desk and when Galen came in did not look up. Galen stood in front of the desk in an easy pose, as though he were only standing there to watch Maulnier's long-fingered hand move across a paper. After a moment, and still without lifting his head, Maulnier said,

" You would do better to ask directly for anything you want."

" I don't understand you," Galen said gently.

" You want a permit to be out after curfew tonight." Maulnier looked up quickly. " Why tonight ? "

" I had arranged to spend the evening with the Baron von Altdorf, my wife's cousin. He's busy during the day. It's a question of an estate, a legacy."

" Why ask a woman, and that particular woman, to get it for you ? I'm not a politician."

" I'm still rather in the dark," Galen said, smiling. " I suppose your English officer has been encouraging my sister-in-law to make herself interesting. I can't forbid it. Perhaps you don't entirely control the movements of an English officer."

Maulnier moved his head, to shake off the last sentence. " It's not possible to give you a permit for tonight. To-morrow if you like."

" I'm very much obliged, but I won't trouble you for tomorrow." Galen waited. " May I go ? " he said at last.

There was a silence. " Sit down," Maulnier said.

" You're very kind." Galen seated himself.

The French officer leaned back. He left it to his shoulders to mark that the conversation had taken a friendly turn ; his voice was still curt. " I'm going to ask an indiscreet and brutally frank question. Is there something brewing in the village — or in the district ? "

" But surely everything is quiet ? "

" Too quiet. . . . I've been in charge of a district in Africa, Colonel von Galen. I've felt a calm like this, just before the most unpleasant trouble I ever had with savages."

Galen smiled. " And you feel that you are living among savages here ? " he murmured.

" No. But — I'll be frank with you — I've always felt that there is something irrational — if I were speaking to anyone else, I should say, something hysterical or primitive — very close to the surface in Germany. Even here, in the most European part of the country."

" The most civilised," Galen said, gently ironical.

" This part of Germany has been exposed to French influence for centuries," Maulnier said with complete calm.

After a moment the German said quietly, " I should say that everything is normal."

" You have no suspicions ? "

" And if I had," Galen said in the same voice, " you would expect me, an officer, like yourself, to denounce a German to you ? "

Maulnier shrugged his shoulders slightly. " Nothing of the sort. . . . You had a great deal to say about peaceful relations. You even offered a, what was it ?, a pact. A loyal pact."

" Which you refused," Galen smiled.

The other swept the air in front of him with his hand. " As you please."

The German said very slowly, " Perhaps you were right — and the division between our countries is too deep. I've seen no signs that you want to make an alliance with us."

" Alliance ? " Maulnier repeated sharply. He sat up.

" I used an old-fashioned word. I only meant by it that you need us as much as we need you. Our two countries complement each other to a quite incredible degree. We're the Siamese twins of Europe — you all balance and repose, we all restlessness, hysteria you would say, energy. Our cradles are too full and yours too empty. You, with your delightfully careless perfection, had, before this war, reached a peak of civilised living it would have been our duty to protect from the awful mechanised molochs on each side of you. . . . I mean Russia and America, of course."

The French colonel leaned back again, at his ease. " Exactly as a millionaire might take a charming girl under his protection. Thanks."

" Do you know, you're quite fatally wrong. France will destroy herself in trying to become a great power. If I may say so, France is a spirit. A spiritual power."

" I admit that we are still weak," Maulnier said in a meditative voice. " But we've paid — paid in advance — by the torture you put us through — for our strength. And we shall get it."

" I hope so," the German said politely.

" You Germans bought your victory over us with an atrocious cruelty," Maulnier said. He paused. " I'm talking as a soldier," he went on quietly, " not as a moralist. . . . You paid shamefully for it, but are you ashamed ? Not in the least. I often wonder whether you have learned anything. Except to plot more cleverly, and fight — when we allow you to fight us again — even more mercilessly."

Galen only smiled. " How well you know our weaknesses."

" I intend that one district in Germany — mine — shall be fit to live in," Maulnier said drily.

" You have the means."

An inflection in Galen's voice, always so quiet, and not

very distinct, suggested that he was going on. But he was silent.

" I should like you to say what is in your mind," Maulnier said at last.

" You are ambitious, my dear sir. You want to make a success here," Galen said softly.

Maulnier answered him with perfect simplicity. " Of course. I'm a professional soldier. . . . I'm also determined to do anything one man can to make another of these bloody struggles between us impossible."

Galen leaned forward. He seemed suddenly to have forgotten that he was a poor devil of a civilian : even to his voice he had grown more rigid.

" You don't believe me, but no one is more convinced than I am that they are ruinous. They ought not to happen. . . . Everything I say is vitiated by the mistakes we made. We're bad diplomatists — we Germans. It's no use my repeating that you yourselves are making just such a fatal mistake now. There's only one hope for the future, and that's for us to become friends, yes, friends. With just a little more goodwill we could have had a friendship which left both of us free to show off our natural virtues. You would have civilised us, and we should have recharged you with our crude energy. . . . We could have been friends on those terms — honourable to both of us——"

He had more to say, but Maulnier interrupted him. " We don't care for such friendships," he said with energy. " They're nothing of the kind. Friendship is only possible between equals ; so far the only equality between us has been that of our dead young men after a war." Abruptly, he stopped, pushed his chair back and stood up. He walked a few paces. Galen had risen at once, and Maulnier turned back, almost turned on him. " We're your superiors now — thanks to the way you behaved in France," he said

ironically. " One of my officers — Aubrac — is very much
your superior. He has survived the worst you can do to
anyone. And he finds you ridiculous, you know."

Galen's face changed quickly. " I'm sorry," he said
with a half-suppressed rage, " he's the type of Frenchman
I can't stand. Insolent and malicious——"

" Quite." Maulnier almost smiled. " I'm not the
Frenchman you have to persuade to make friends with you.
The day you forgive Aubrac for having mutilated him by
torture — and the day when he decides to respect you for
your modest efficiency as a farmer, or a scientist, or an
architect — anything you like except a murderer — that will
be the first day of real peace. Until then . . ."

Galen had controlled himself. He said gently, " Until
then you won't trust me."

" It isn't necessary. We trust ourselves," Maulnier said
swiftly. He hesitated. " You can go."

" Thanks for your patience with me," Galen said.

Maulnier let him get as far as the door. " Wait." Sitting
down at the desk, he wrote for a minute, then held the
slip of paper at arm's length. " Your permit for tonight,"
he said curtly.

" I'm extraordinarily grateful to you," the German said
warmly. He took the paper, with a slight smile, and went
out.

As soon as he was alone, Maulnier got up and walked
to a mirror : half smiling, he adjusted the belt on his thin
waist. Aubrac came in, with Adrian Long ; turning to them,
he said,

" He's not a bad chap, von Galen. Pity he's a Boche."

" I should be much sorrier if he were French," Aubrac
exclaimed.

Maulnier frowned. " He's a good soldier."

" And vain, and portentous, and convinced of his mission

to sleep with the universe," Aubrac said.

He had seated himself at one of the tables, in the attitude he would have taken if it had been the iron table of a café. He looked up with an ironical smile. "Are they brave? I suppose so — if a man who is so frightened of dying that he commits suicide is brave. They must be horribly frightened to try as desperately as they do to make the world safe for Germans. Only Germans. I suspect them of being deathly afraid of each other — look at the ghastly way Germans have always treated Germans. It's their endless cold nights, and the cold summers, which aren't summers, and the muddy light. A hill in France is a hill, you can see it and build a house on it, and our rivers are rivers, where you fish. Here you'd probably hook some yelling Rhine-maiden or other. . . . What was I saying? Yes, all that cold and darkness, and the hatreds it bred, and the revolting stories they made up and told each other — no wonder they're alarmed by themselves, no wonder they have these manias about obedience and duty, and no wonder they periodically blow the lid off to prove how strong they are and to get rid of their nightmares. Then the rest of us have to kill ourselves to put them back where they came from, and that's another nightmare, and when they're not crying themselves to sleep over it, poor little Hansels and Gretels, they're plotting with our late allies — I don't mean you, Adrian. . . ." So much for my own nightmare, he thought bitterly, with the bitterness he had kept out of his voice: the Russians will make a firm bloc with the Boches, and the two together will fall on us. . . . "And what a bore it all is," he added, smiling. "You wait — one of these times they'll bore us to death."

The colonel had paused again in front of the mirror on his way to the door. "Don't worry. God will always save France."

Aubrac's eyes sparkled. " Do you expect Him to do as much for the English, sir ? "

With a cold politeness Maulnier said, " The English are generally in a position to look after themselves, they have made a habit of it."

He went out. Long glanced after him with an amused smile, but when he turned expectantly to Aubrac — the joke, Maulnier's polite dislike of the English, was familiar — he was silenced by the look, half ironical, half inquisitive, on Aubrac's face. The silence lasted fully a minute, then Aubrac said, slowly, with indifference,

" I was thinking . . . are you happy here ? "

" Happy enough."

Aubrac looked at him. " You're able to amuse yourself.'

" What are you getting at ? " — the Englishman's friendly voice took the edge off his phrase.

Aubrac smiled quickly. Too quick, his smile risked being taken for a grimace. " I like you very much, Adrian — especially your habit of writing poetry on the back of my laundry list. Not bad. Your semi-colons are charming.'

He held out the slip of paper. Pocketing it, Long said " Thanks. . . . Didn't you notice the comma in line two ? "

" You're too damned young. Why didn't you go home and begin living ? "

" I'm twenty-six. A little old to begin."

" You've had six years of the army. Only an Englishman could still be so — I hope it's not an insult — so innocent.'

" You and I had different wars."

" True."

There was a silence. Aubrac stared in front of him. Without their gleam of malicious irony, his eyes were only restless. Long waited, and at last, with affection, said " You can say what you like."

" A German woman is one thing," Aubrac said quietly

d slowly — " I don't care for them myself, too like an
fficial handbook of the womanly virtues, but for your sake
you'd fallen for one of them I'd have done my best. . . .
ut a young Frenchwoman who could marry a German,
a moment when other French girls were being obscenely
andled — I know what I'm saying . . . an inexcusable
ck of taste — not even bad taste. . . . You'd certainly
islike it when she drifted into some minor crime, murder
r incest."

" Do you believe in punishing a young woman all her
fe for a mistake which injured only her ? " Long said
ntly. " She suffered, no one else did."

Aubrac's bitterness distorted his sunken face. " A mis-
ke ? . . . Suppose she were English, not French ? It's
asy to be forgiving at a distance. Suppose you remembered
me girl rather well, a narrow pale face and long hair,
e next time you hear about her she has been tortured to
eath, she'd picked up a few inches of English parachute
rd and made a belt of it. . . . Well ? "

The young Englishman shook his head with a smiling
bstinacy. " I can't suppose Marie anything but French."

" Oh my God, what do you know about the French ? "
ubrac said, with despair and mockery.

" They are intelligent and human, they smile when other
omen would be seeing themselves as tragic figures, they
e obstinate, their hands are a little too short, but other
omen's hands are too long in comparison, they know
erything about living without knowing it, they have no
oism and the least possible vanity."

Aubrac threw his hands up. " You're lost ! "

He stopped abruptly as Colonel Maulnier came back into
e room. At the same moment, a slight disturbance began
itside the room, on the landing. A clear unflurried voice,
arie's. . . . *But you must tell them I'm here ; I must speak*

to one of the officers, it's urgent. . . .

Maulnier stiffened with annoyance and disgust. " Orde
that woman off," he said to his adjutant.

Aubrac limped to the door and opened it. Marie's ar₩
was held tightly by the sentry. She was not trying to fr₭
herself.

" It would be kind of you not to make a nuisance ₡
yourself, Frau von Leyde."

The young woman looked at him without any sign th₃
she noticed his contempt. " You know I shouldn't con
here unless it were important," she said quietly. " Despe₩
ately important."

Colonel Maulnier had his back to the door. He turne₫
round. " Major Aubrac — you'll tell Colonel von Gale
tomorrow morning that he and his family must go."

Looking at him directly, Marie said, " You had bett₭
leave him where you can keep an eye on him."

Maulnier continued to stare at her, with the cold pen₭
trating glance he had taught himself as a young man : s₭
endured it with what seemed to him a blasphemous eas₭
but he could not pretend that she was impudent as we₦
" Bring her in," he said after a moment.

He sat down behind the desk and watched her as sh₭
walked quickly across the room. She stood in front of hin₭
" Now," he said curtly. " What is it ? "

She was much less calm than she had seemed, and sh₭
began to speak agitatedly : it exasperated his disapprov₃
and distaste, and he regretted that he had let her in : sh₭
has prepared some scene, he thought.

" I came to tell you — the English politicians who a₭
arriving tonight in Mainz are not safe ; they are going t₭
try to kill them. You must do something quickly."

As I thought, he said to himself. " What is all this ? "
he asked drily.

" The Englishmen, the members of parliament," she said urgently, " there's a plot of some sort, or an ambush — I can't tell you when it will happen or where, I don't know, I only know that there *is* a plot, and Colonel von Galen knows about it. . . . Please believe me."

Unmoved, he said, " Where did you pick up this story ? "

" Don't you understand what I'm saying ? They're coming tonight, and someone, somewhere, will try to kill them. . . . Do you — you can't want it to happen ? " She stepped back from the desk, looking at him with horror. " What in God's name are you doing ? "

In spite of himself, Maulnier had begun to lose his certainty that she was untrustworthy, a natural liar, or had made the thing up for her own purposes, to gain sympathy — a double traitor — why not ?

" If you'll be good enough to give me some details, Frau von Leyde. . . ."

She forced herself to speak calmly. " I have told you everything I know."

" Who is going to attack them ? "

" I don't know."

" Where ? "

" I only know what I have told you."

Maulnier leaned forward. He spoke in a coldly correct voice, almost as though she were a fellow officer whom he disliked. " You're asking me to believe that someone, you don't know who, is going at some moment, you don't know when or where, to assassinate these Englishmen, but you don't know how. Is that all you wanted to say ? "

His manner to her had hardened Marie : she replied as coldly, " Yes, that's all."

Aubrac spoke for the first time. " The special train with these people is due at midnight," he said quietly.

" In six and a half hours," Marie said in a dry voice.

" Wait over there," Maulnier said to her.

She went quickly to the back of the room, and stood there, near Long. Without seeming to, Aubrac watched them closely, but they did not glance at one another. The colonel, who was writing, said curtly,

" Captain Long."

Long came across to the desk. " Ring up Second Bureau at Command, ask for Colonel Thomas and give him the message. Himself." He held out the slip of paper. " Come back here."

Long left the room, and without turning his head Maulnier said sharply, " Frau von Leyde."

" Yes," the young woman drawled.

" I want to know where you heard this."

" I can't tell you that."

" Come here, please."

She came back to the desk, moving with her light step. Aubrac watched.

" I want to know the names of the conspirators — besides Colonel von Galen."

" I don't think Colonel von Galen is responsible," she said quietly. " I think he may be trying to prevent it — of course he would do his best to keep you from finding out. . . . Or he may be helpless. He wouldn't be responsible for such a frightful thing."

Eyeing her, Maulnier leaned back. " Why not ? "

She made a light gesture, lifting both hands, palm upward, as if she were displaying Galen's innocence, but her voice gave away her anxiety. She had persuaded herself that he was innocent, but, facing the two men who were her judges as well as his, she felt uncertain. Not only of him. A deep uncertainty had invaded her spirit ; just when she needed them most, her carefully-composed defences had failed and she was confused and weak. The one thing that supported her was their contempt; she clung to it, each time she felt its touch she was hardened to go on. Yes, but where? I am in France, she said to herself; this is the cold of France. She made an effort to speak with assurance.

"You've seen him yourself, and talked to him. It's impossible for him to talk as he does — reasonable, hating the shootings and those things — and kind — and to be planning a murder. It's absolutely impossible."

The colonel nodded. "I should have said he was talking in good faith . . . yes," he said, less to her than to himself.

Aubrac suddenly flung his arm out. It caught a hand-lamp standing on a table and sent it to roll, broken and clattering, across the floor. He seemed not to notice it.

"A German who is not a brute always acts in good faith. Doesn't he?" he said with an implacable bitterness. "He offers, all in good faith, to marry you and make a good use of your dowry; and when you refuse the offer he begins to kill and torture you with the same innocent self-righteousness. My God, if one thing has ruined Europe, it is the unbelievable and intolerable good faith of the Germans. No mere scoundrel ever did such damage."

"Nonsense, nonsense — what nonsense," Maulnier said in a sharp voice. "If a man is a sincere idealist he's not a murderer——"

"Colonel von Galen, sir, is a German."

"—unless he's insane."

Aubrac's pallor had suddenly become alarming. "They *are* such crashing bores, these Germans. All this nonsense about dying in war, and the glories of conquest. Lunacy. German lunacy. If they could once realise how they bore everyone. . . ."

"Yes, yes, Michel," his colonel said gently. Aubrac sat down.

Marie had listened with a feeling that was neither pity nor horror, it was a claw of both : pity alone would be impudence. When Maulnier spoke to her, with less formality and a more marked contempt than usual, she felt only relief.

" You refuse to tell us the names of the conspirators. Very well. I shall arrest all your family and question them in front of you."

" Just as you like," she said firmly. " I can't tell you anything more."

Aubrac lifted his head. " That gets Frau von Leyde into trouble——"

" I daresay it will," Maulnier said with indifference. He frowned. " What a devil of a time it is taking that fellow to get through to Command."

" She has put herself in a certain amount of danger, sir," Aubrac said slowly.

Maulnier yawned. " It seems to me that she has done the only thing she could — and she hasn't done it very well."

There was no longer any confusion in Marie's mind, she was calm and lucid. It is not because I am what I am, she thought, that he is behaving with this callousness ; he would have been just as callous without an excuse : he is a successful soldier.

Aubrac said lightly, " Do you think perhaps, sir, it might be worth while postponing another outbreak of French brutality and shamelessness ? After all, it's not impossible that von Galen is innocent — comparatively. If we can avoid telling him that we suspect him, and have him watched — we may lay our hands on a great many other people. Possibly more important."

" And trust this woman, with her disorderly habits, to hold her tongue ? " Maulnier said.

" You can probably trust her as far as that," Aubrac said deliberately.

Had he looked at Marie, he would have had the satisfaction of seeing that this insult, following his move to save her, had wounded her more deeply than Maulnier's coldness, far more deeply. She gripped the edge of the desk. The door opened, and Captain Long came in.

" Did you speak to Colonel Thomas ? "

" Yes, sir."

" Right." He glanced briefly at Marie. " You can go now. But hold your tongue."

She did not move. She was realising in this moment her helplessness and the grimness of what was going to happen. " What have I done ? " she said under her breath.

" Informed us," Maulnier said drily, " that certain members of your family are scoundrels — of the usual sort."

The excitement you feel when the worst happens and you are ruined made her light-headed and gave her an astonishing feeling of energy and, yes, hope. " You are a Frenchman of the usual sort," she said, hardly able not to smile, " you argue very logically in circles : they bring you back where you started, which proves how right you were all the time. . . . It's very likely I've given away to you the one man who was trying to stop the crime. . . . And might stop it."

Maulnier leaned forward again, so that she should miss nothing of his intimidating glance. " Did you hear him talk about it yourself ? "

" No."

" The name of your informant ? "

She was silent. Major Aubrac had turned away, but the Englishman watched her anxiously.

" It's you, Frau von Leyde, who are forcing me to arrest all of them."

" Very well," she said calmly. " Are you going to lock me in with them ? "

" Naturally — since you're all Germans, I shall put you all together," he said icily.

Marie smiled. " And what happens if they kill me ? "

" What should happen ? "

" Or if I kill myself first ? "

" Why should that interest me ? " he said in a dry voice.

" Your only witness ? " she mocked him.

He lifted his eyebrows. " Why should you imagine that coming here to inform against your relations gives you the right to try to bargain with us ? "

" I shouldn't dream of bargaining," she smiled. " Anything you could offer me, from your side, would only be egoism, callousness, a narrow religion and a wide, an absolutely limitless ambition."

" You can go," Maulnier said after a moment.

Long held the door open for her : she went out without looking at him.

3

She ran down the stone stairs and along the passage to the kitchen : her despairing excitement drove her to open the door without listening outside it. If she were seen coming through this door from the French wing she was ruined — but ruin was a matter of an hour or minutes : why take any care ? When she walked into an empty room she almost felt disappointed. She went quickly to the mantelpiece and took down the miniature of her husband : an impulse she did not want to understand had sent her to it — but she felt only a cold pity, no regret, not even a twinge of shame. " You would have died here, Jeannot. One way or another you would have died," she

id, smiling. " Of disappointment — or you would have
hanged and become two men, and I should never have
nown which of you I was touching. Nowadays no German
an live and be sane. . . . Think—" suddenly she noticed
he blueness of the eyes — " no, I daren't think," she said
naudibly. She put the miniature down. Her feeling of
xcitement left her ; she was only tired. She stood in the
middle of the room, trying with a little anguish to think
hat she ought to do in these last few moments.

There was a light knock, and Captain Long came into
he room. She felt a shock of anger — he was going to
estroy her calm — and said,

" You have no right to be here. This is a German room.
What do you want ? "

In the instant, as she was speaking, the room turned
s back on her, with a rudeness Bertha von Leyde would
ave approved, which said sourly : You yourself have no
ght here. . . . No, she thought quickly, I have no right.
ut where can I go ?

" The colonel is not going to arrest your brother-in-law,"
ong said quietly. " Not yet. He told us as soon as you
ft. . . . You're not involved."

" Would it have mattered ? " she said with real indiffer-
nce.

" Yes, I think so. Your brother-in-law's friends would
robably have shot you, they would say you are a traitor."

He had spoken gently, watching her ; she was sur-
rised by the warm confidence his voice gave her. It
as not like the tension between them earlier, she felt
othing of that tormented pleasure : this was lighter and
appy. Everything had become easy. . . . She could not
elp ruining the seriousness of the moment. How ridiculous,
t any time, to take Marie von Leyde, Marie Jouvenet,
eriously.

" So I am," she said, smiling. " My trouble is to know which country to betray to the other. Both dislike me as much as I deserve. . . . I'm sure I shall live to be a hundred. I'm horribly strong."

" You're not safe here," Long said.

" I'm glad," she said simply. " I've had too much safety, more than the other girls in my village. I shall be lucky if having a short life makes me exactly like them again."

" And you used to tell me you are a German ! "

" I daren't think what I am," she said gravely.

" You're no more at home in this room than I am. You don't wish you had been called Brunhilde, you're sensible and ordinary."

She smiled, because to cry would be helpless and ugly. " I'm glad you think I'm sensible. . . . Goodbye. Thank you for coming to tell me."

" Are you trying to get rid of me ? "

Now she wanted him to go — she was afraid ; at any moment someone might come in. " Yes, you must go," she said firmly.

He did not move. " I really came to ask you to marry me. No — don't speak. Let me tell you something first — I'm nobody. My father makes a very good cloth — tweed if you know what that is. He used to have an agent in Paris — I learned French with him. Now he wants me back, I mean my father, and I'm going home to be released. The order recalling me came into the office when I was telephoning just now. I was expecting it. . . . You can speak now, my darling."

She saw that his hands were shaking, and felt a foolish wish to take hold of them to comfort him. She said frankly, " I knew you would ask me."

" Good."

" I was going to refuse. I had the sentence ready, it

was rather long but polite and very touching, you would have been touched."

Long smiled at her. " Try it on me."

Her joy choked her, but she made herself speak lightly. " No."

" Marie ! "

Holding him away from her, she said, " I love you."

" I love you, Marie," he said gently.

" No, no, this isn't the way," she cried. " Argue with me. Try to convince me I have the right to marry you. It's not true, but I should be glad if it were."

" I warn you I'm tired. . . . Five — nearly six years of the war have taught me how useful it is to have illusions, and taken most of mine from me. I know now that I'm not going to do anything remarkable — in fact, I don't want to. Nowadays I haven't the energy or the persistence. You might resent this, you know. I'm not offering you much — you'd better think twice ! "

" You're not offering me anything but honesty, intelligence, kindness — a long happy life. . . . I wish terribly that you were ill or hideous, or that you had been spoiled."

With a half-suppressed vehemence — it startled her — Long said, " I should loathe it if I had had to be pitied."

She had a hateful feeling that things were going wrong, she had said the wrong things or disappointed him in some way. " If either of us needs pity, don't you think I do ? . . . To have nothing good enough for you."

" Neither of us needs it. Why should we, we've had the marvellous luck to drop on each other while we're young — time to live and all that. Our grandmothers would have said it was meant. If anything these days means anything we're going to have superb lives."

" No ! " she said, terrified. " No, my darling, no, no, no. Don't say it."

' What ? "

" The only sort of life I want is one nobody can notice or envy. Perfectly dull and quiet. A long dull boring life. Promise me."

He smiled suddenly, a young confident smile. " I'll do my best. . . . Very well, it's settled."

He was very close to her now, looking at her with a warning gravity.

" No — wait," she said — she was afraid of her joy.

" I'll come back for you," Long said. " I suppose it will take me all of three months to get out of the army and get permission to come back and fetch you. Can you bear it ? We'll be married in England, and once a year we'll spend a month in France to melt the ice off our bones. Three months — it's a hell of a long time. I'll write to you every week."

She shook her head. " You can't write to me."

" Why not ? "

" What do you think would become of me here if I had letters coming every week from England ? " she said lightly. She was determined to make things seem easy and normal. " I should be denounced."

" Haven't you any friends I could write to ? "

" Friends ? I have Heinrich and Anna."

" My poor love ! " he stammered, in horrified realisation of her life.

" It's perfectly simple," she smiled. " I'll write to you once a week and answer the questions you ask me in the dozens of letters you can't write. I'll go on writing for three months, and then another month. If you're still silent, I shall know you've changed your mind, you're not coming."

" I shall come."

He had moved close to her again, and she evaded him

with a quick movement. It was not coquetry. It was the fear she had all along been suppressing, trying to suppress. He is too young, she told herself with anguish : he is four years older than I am and he's a child, an honest child. She knew what she ought to say, and made her voice as colourless as possible.

" And your family ? They won't forgive me when they have to explain to their neighbours why your French wife was living here. You'll hate it when they despise me."

" You don't explain yourself to the neighbours in England," he said quietly, " and no one I care tuppence about will despise my wife."

Before she could stop herself she had cried, " Don't say it."

" What's wrong, what have I said ? "

She was silent.

Long turned pale — as though his pain were a physical one : no doubt it was, since jealousy, the most hideous emotion any human being ever suffers, has nothing to do with the mind. Or not at first.

" Oh, I see. That was what *he* said to you," he managed to say calmly.

" The terrible thing is that it's done," she said with despair. " I would do anything to put it right, and there's nothing I can do, nothing. Nothing. . . . I'm ashamed."

" He gave you your first happiness," Long said drily.

She forgot herself in her need to comfort him. " You see, my darling — you wouldn't be able to stand it. I told you so. . . ." She went on in a gay voice : " And now you must really go. It's marvellous of you to want to marry me, it comforts my vanity and makes me proud. I refuse you — with all the gratitude in the world. I shall never forget it."

Long's face changed, it became smooth and candid —

" Now you're talking nonsense. . . . Provided I have you
I can stand anything."

" But that's not what I want. . . . I only want the
simplest things. To have breakfast with you, to pass you
the jar of honey, to wear an old dress so cleverly that you
admire me in it — only the everyday boring joys. No
storms of jealousy and reconciliation. I don't want our
lives to be dramatic."

" They won't be. Listen," he said, smiling, and trembling
a little, " we've been married fifty years already, we're far
past making scenes with each other, when you are in the
wrong I apologise to you and you forgive me, that's all."

" Really only fifty years ? It seems longer. Was I
always impatient ? When I broke things and said it was
your fault, and scolded you, what did you do ? "

" I put my arms round you."

" Like this ? "

" Yes, like this."

She tried to say, " And then ? " but Long kissed her
mouth. After a minute, bewildered with pleasure, she said
foolishly, " Yes, it's true."

" It's true that we can stand anything," he said gently.

" You see, you're not tired."

" All the same, we won't go in for storms, we'll have a
very quiet life."

Closing her eyes, she saw a large shabby room, its
windows open on a small and very neat garden : unlike her
school friends, for whom the word England called up an
image of wealth, pedigree dogs, and rain, she never saw
anything except the sun showing up the worn places in
chairs and rugs, and, at best, a friendly mongrel. It was
these she was going to — and to obscurity, safety, happiness.

" If ever two people were thankful to be like everyone

else, to be nobody, we'll be. And content — and obedient. And happy."

Long smiled. "Now it's you who are tempting the fates."

"I'm too insignificant, they can't see me."

"You know, don't you, that I shall come back."

She knew he meant : Since we were able to live in that hell of jealousy we can survive anything. His jealousy had been as deep as her shame and degradation, they had been reconciled below that depth ; they were safe. "Yes, yes, I'm sure you'll come," she said.

Long put his hand on her shoulder. This barely friendly gesture delighted her, and she turned her head to kiss his hand. Major Aubrac came in. He stood in the doorway and looked at them, holding the door open.

"You asked me for five minutes," he said in a flat voice. "The old man has just sent for you."

"Right." Long turned away from her and moved towards the door. She noticed that Aubrac was looking at her, not at Long. What is he hoping for ? she said to herself. That I shall protest or cry ? She smiled.

"One minute — less than that — ten seconds — is as long as anyone needs to ruin himself for life," Aubrac said with his travesty of politeness.

In spite of herself she blushed. "Have I ruined your friend ?"

"I don't blame you. You have every right to run away," he said.

Long turned round. "Until tomorrow, Marie."

"Yes, yes, tomorrow," she said gaily.

She went over to the door Aubrac had shut behind them and leaned on it lightly, spreading her arms out. Instead of the anguish she had felt a moment ago, the moment when Long turned from her, she was shaken by a delicious joy. It made her want to laugh, cry, dance. She started at a loud heavy noise of steps outside the other door. It was thrown open and Heinrich came in.

"I came for that book." He looked at her angrily. "You said you got it for me as well. Where is it?"

Crossing the room to open a cupboard, she took the book from the back of one of the shelves. "Here. Where you put it yourself. Take it and keep it in your room."

"Don't you mind my keeping it?"

"Of course not." She stretched her arms again, smiling. "What a lovely day!"

"Do you think so?" He did not know what he suspected — except that she was cheating him in some way.

"There hasn't been such a day all the year. Not a cloud. Didn't you notice the leaves this morning, gossiping like old women — it's a sure sign of a fine day. And the sun. No one could be unlucky on a day like this."

"Unless he misses them," Heinrich muttered.

She did not hear him. "What did you say?"

"Nothing. . . . You seem pleased with yourself. Why?"

"Do you really want to see the Loire," she said, caressing him lightly, "and eat an omelette with sorrel in it?"

"Not if you're not going to be there."

"I might — it's just possible I might be." She could not help laughing.

"Is that true — do you promise?" he said, half ready to believe her.

"Why not?" She moved quickly to the door. "I've been thinking of that sorrel omelette for years. Years and months. I'm starving!"

"Marie," the boy shouted. "Don't go without me."

"Silly, I'm going to my room—" she blew him a kiss. In the instant of closing the door she heard a curious sound she could hardly have guessed that Heinrich had thrown

e Ronsard on the floor and was stamping on it. After a
oment he stopped and, blinking to shake the tears of rage
om his eyelashes, bent down and picked it up.

Chapter Four

I

HE village next morning — without a single person
ving left or come in since the day before, and without
wspapers or a train — was alive with rumours, all of them
ecise and very alarming. Towards midday Richard Gauss
ought them with him to the château, into the kitchen,
d recited them with less than his usual awkwardness to
tte, her mother, and Heinrich. The table was set for
nch with the small dishes of cold vegetables, salad, and
raps of liver-sausage and salami, only scraps — they
oked well because Anna's clumsy fingers had arranged
em skilfully.

" I knew something had happened when they stopped
e trains as far back as Cologne. The poor old Winters
ere on the platform for eight hours — afraid to go back
me because they had told everyone about their holiday
d Frau Winter had borrowed a petticoat. Their neigh-
urs must have died of laughing."

" Serve them right," Lotte said loudly. " Why should
l people have holidays ? Let them stay at home."

Bertha von Leyde was examining the dishes : food had
come very important to her : it was not only greed ; her
rld was narrowing again to the moment when all its joys
uld be an infant's, and just as sharp, trivial, and infinitely

absorbing. " How bored I'm going to be without you, r little love," she said mournfully. " Only Anna left — a she is such a fool."

" I'll come in," Lotte said, without turning her hea As well as Anna she knew that their mother had aged many years in the last few weeks : she had even guessed Anna, still afraid of her mother, had not — that Bertha v Leyde, who had seen death come in for others without ever entering her head that she, too, had a death somewhe was afraid of dying. But she did not pity her. How cou she ? There was too much of her mother in her — that of a young Bertha ; who knew nothing, nothing at a about what it is like to be old. She, Lotte, knew that s would never be old . . . and she had nearer things worry about than the griefs of an old woman : she wou be all wife, and all mother, but she was hardly at all daughter, she left that to Anna.

" Did you know there was going to be trouble ? " s asked Richard. Her voice shook a little.

" Oh well, I knew something was up when Colonel v Galen told me to find out for him about the special trair He gave a nervous laugh. " I didn't ask him any questio . . . what do you think ? I'm not a colonel."

" For goodness' sake, call him Paul," Lotte cried. don't see," she went on in an anxious voice, " why y should be dragged in. I'm going to tell Paul to let y alone."

" You daren't," Heinrich said.

The trouble in Lotte's voice had roused her moth With a spurt of rage and energy, she said, " Is this r house or isn't it ? I won't have Paul behaving as thou he were master here. He's not. Things are going on h that I know nothing about. I don't like it. . . ." H pity for herself welled up, drowning her voice. " Y shouldn't leave me, Lotte. Who's going to bring me my coffee in the mornings ? And you know, I have such bad nights — and often bad dreams. I dreamed last night that I was a little girl and my mother was here and she was dying. I was frightened, and I cried, oh, how I cried ! "

" What nonsense," Lotte said with brusque good-humour. " You're still alive."

More comforted by this than she would have been by Anna's gentleness, Bertha turned back to the table. " Yes, I am — and I'm going to look after myself," she said cheerfully. Choosing a piece of salami, she put it quickly and cunningly into her mouth.

" I must go now, Lotte," Richard said in a low voice.

She looked at him with a young anguish. " Take care of yourself. . . . It's absurd, but I feel as though we are being trapped."

" Don't be afraid," he said steadily. " Everything will be all right when we are together. . . ." He turned to the baroness. " Goodbye . . . er, Mamma."

" Goodbye, Richard," Bertha muttered, with her back to him.

Just as they reached the door, it opened : Paul von Galen came in with Anna. " Ah, Richard," he said kindly — a kindness that infuriated his young sister-in-law : she, if Richard did not, knew that he was being patronised — " I want your help. Come and see me when you are off duty tomorrow."

" What do you want with him ? " Lotte asked fiercely.

" Lotte, I am sure you were brought up not to ask questions," Galen smiled.

She did not speak. In the doorway, she gave Richard a brief convulsive embrace, then pushed him out and slammed the door. Heinrich had crept up to her. " What did I tell you ? " he whispered spitefully.

Suddenly Bertha von Leyde startled them with the harsh bullying voice they had not heard from her for weeks — " I have something to say to you, Paul. This is my house and I won't have it turned into a hotel for your friends. You have no right to abuse my kindness. If my husband were alive, you wouldn't dare use his house as if it were your own."

In his gentlest tones her son-in-law answered, " It wouldn't be necessary. Your husband was a patriot."

" My good man, do you suggest I'm not ? " Her eyes held a gleam of rage — but it was only a gleam, and her voice had weakened. When Galen moved towards her she watched him with a defiant nervousness. Taking hold of her by the arm he pushed her gently towards a chair.

" You'll tire yourself, Mamma," he said, " sit down. I don't suggest anything. Except that we all have our duties, and if yours is to see nothing and hear nothing, that doesn't mean you are useless. You are the greatest use — in your place. Do sit down."

Smiling, he pressed her into the chair, and she sat down without another word. She only looked rather pitifully at Anna — who was looking away.

" Father, you must tell us what is happening," Heinrich exclaimed.

His father looked at him with a slight smile. " Why, what is happening ? "

" Don't make fun of me ! I know all about it : you were going to kill all the English, weren't you ? " His voice deepened with a confident admiration and love. " Why don't you let me help you ? I'm old enough now. I can fire a rifle. Let me help."

" You're old enough not to talk like a schoolgirl," Galen said sternly. " Where did you pick up this nonsense ? "

The boy's confidence vanished, and he looked alarmed.

" Everyone knows about it. . . . I don't know."

Before Galen could speak, his wife began one of her distracted remarks. " It's very inconvenient having no trains, Paul. I don't know what we shall do without the nails I ordered, they were coming on the three o'clock ; every stair is a death-trap with the loose carpet. . . . One of us is going to break his neck——" She put her hand over her mouth, as though she had said something unlucky.

Galen patted her shoulder. " Dear Anna ! " he said kindly. He drew himself up, straightening his long back, and began to speak in what Lotte called his professor's voice, didactic and mumbling — as gentle as ever but coldly impersonal, as though he had forgotten that he was talking to a schoolboy and three women.

" I've decided to talk seriously to you all — now — while Marie is out——"

Lotte interrupted him with a malicious shriek. " Oho, what has our dear little Marie done ? "

Galen frowned and ignored her. " I insist on one thing. That you hold your tongues. It is the first lesson a soldier learns, and we are all soldiers. Yes, Heinrich. Your second lesson is to avoid as if it were an electric wire any inquisitiveness and any rumour. Silence anyone who tries to repeat gossip or foolish questions. And don't expect that you will ever understand more about things than I choose to tell you — or than some other person tells you in my name if I am arrested. Or shot. One reason why I am talking to you is to put an end once and for all to the most shameful of children's vices — curiosity."

He gave a violent start, his head jerking backwards. Heinrich had knocked a cup off the table with his elbow ; it broke noisily on the stone floor. " Don't fidget ! " he shouted.

" He's a child, Paul," his wife said faintly.

Heinrich had flushed scarlet. He sprang round on hi
mother in a fury. " That's not true — I'm a man now
Women are liars and cowards, all of them. I heard yo
say Thank God, when Lotte told you the Englishmen hadn'
come—" he turned to his father and said in a quiete
trusting voice, " You can't rely on women, but you can o
me, you know. You can tell me to do anything. Th
harder the better. . . ."

Galen was calm again. He looked in an amused wa
at his son, and talked with smiling gestures, more tha
ever like a don : so like that you expected him to prov
by syllogisms that reason, goodwill, a balanced mind
are marks of insanity, and that the same gentle smile i
equal to two things which differ absurdly, civility an
murder.

" Yes, yes — let me finish what I want to say. . . . On
of you may be small-minded enough — or merely selfis
— to want peace at any price, a mean little peace in he
own house. Such people will be disappointed. If ther
is to be reconciliation, as the English say, the world mus
be reconciled to us, not Germany to the world. We ar
shamefully weak now, weaker, as the old women say, tha
a babe unborn, we have to move an inch at a time. W
have to eliminate our traitors. We have to prevent a fals
peace, even if it costs us a few unofficial executions. Th
united nations, as they call themselves officially, must b
worn down and tricked. You've seen birds running awa
from their nests making a great fuss. We must do that
After a time we shall be foxes and double back on ou
tracks. And then we shall be wounded tigers — eh
Heinrich ? . . . You don't like it, Mamma, do you
when I praise Russia—" Bertha von Leyde started, he
heavy cheeks quivered and she looked at him pitifully —
" the mere idea of a German Soviet makes you shiver,'

he said genially. . . . "But what's it matter what I call the whip I use to discipline a dog ? . . . Nothing matters except the reality of power. On the day when the united Soviets of Germany and Russia spring on the world, you'll see something the world has never seen yet . . . irresistible power . . . in a week all will be over——"

He checked himself with a half smile, and waved his hand, excusing himself for having stumbled into enthusiasm. In a barely articulate voice his wife said,

" And then shall we have peace ? "

" As soon as Russia has been subdued, we shall have peace everlasting. *Pax Teutonica*, eh, Heinrich ? " He looked with a quizzical smile at Lotte, who said sullenly,

" Will my children live in it ? "

Bertha von Leyde made an effort to show that she approved of his ruthless patriotism — as indeed she did, but without grasping what he had said. She recognised the fume of sacrifice rising from the altar, that was really all. " You ought to have had Johann here, Paul. . . . Well, you have our good little Heinrich — if his mother hasn't spoiled him."

" You'll see when the time comes," Heinrich said under his breath.

Galen was still smiling at his young sister-in-law, his head on one side : he seemed at this moment fond of her — " Lotte, my dear, your Richard is not very intelligent, but he is brave and reliable."

She did not speak, but his wife said in a whisper — she must have been talking to herself — " No, it's terrible. I despair."

" Anna, Anna," he said kindly.

She turned her head to him like a dog obeying the master he fears more than he loves. " I shall always do everything you want me to, Paul. But if you fail what will become of us ? "

" If I fail I shall kill you and Heinrich, and then kill myself," he said, smiling. The boy ran to him and threw his arms round him, hitting his head against his father's chest. Galen caressed him. " And now let's be sensible."

Lotte asked him in a dry voice, " But what happened yesterday ? You haven't told us."

" Nothing. The train with the English politicians in it was stopped at Coblenz and sent back. Someone behaved treacherously."

" Who ? " Heinrich asked. He took a step away from his father and looked at him.

" That's exactly what we have to find out."

" You don't think it was Marie ? " the boy said uneasily.

After a moment Galen said coldly, " I never judge anyone without evidence."

His wife made a horrified sound. " Paul. . . . What are you going to do ? "

" Why, Anna, you're trembling," he said gently. " Don't be so foolish, my dear. . . . You must behave naturally when Marie is here. She may be quite innocent."

" She's such an awful liar," Heinrich said loudly.

" Heinrich ! " his mother murmured.

" She'll say anything and accuse anyone, to save herself," the boy stuttered.

He broke off sharply. The door was opening, and as Marie came in everyone turned to look at her. She was carrying her heavy basket as though it were part of a ballet.

" I'm sorry I'm late," she said, " it's another marvellous day." No one spoke, but she was used to that ; she went on in the same voice, " I never saw so many happy people as there are in the village this morning. Even the goats were smiling."

Indignation gave Bertha back her vigour. " I don't

elieve it," she said angrily. " In a defeated country,
appiness is a disgrace."

" You're wrong, Mamma," Marie told her, smiling.
They're happy because they're alive and warm. It's the
thers who have been defeated."

Lotte's sullenness had turned, at the sight of her French
ster-in-law, to a mocking dislike. She said spitefully,
She's happy because the French have just arrested every
udent in Mainz."

" I didn't know that ! " Marie cried. " Why ? "

" Why do they lock up our young men ? Because all
heir own are diseased and rotten ! "

Marie looked relieved. So it was nonsense. . . . " I
fuse to quarrel with you, it's too fine a day. Don't you
gree, Anna ? "

Anna made a blind gesture. " Yes. . . . Yes, it's fine."

As she passed Heinrich, Marie spoke in his ear. " After
nch I'll race you three times round the park. I shall
at you."

He did not answer. But his grandmother had caught
rt of the sentence and she said drily, " Heinrich has
mething better to do than run about after you, Marie."

" My dear Marie," Galen said kindly, " you won't realise
at you're in a country where it's not respectable to waste
me. You may take a sun-bath, but you mustn't go out
erely to enjoy the sun, that's inefficient and trivial."

She gave him a grateful look. " Thank you, Paul."

" Well," he said, looking round him with a friendly smile,
let's break bread together, as they say." He leaned over
s wife as she stumbled towards a chair, and settled her
it ; when the others had seated themselves at the table
took the chair next her. " What's the gossip in the
llage, Marie ? "

Marie laughed. " The same scandals. No one knows

how or where Frau Meyer is able to get face-powder, a
it seems to be really true that the chemist's wife kept
bottle of brandy hidden all during the war and only broug
it out yesterday for his funeral. Oh, one new scandal th
I discovered myself, and kept quiet about. Our postmas
went into Mainz yesterday for an hour, and he's s
there."

"But surely you know why?" Galen said. "The
were no trains through yesterday evening or this morning

"Really? They didn't tell me."

"I'm surprised if they're talking of anything else. N
letters, no fresh bread. It's a major tragedy!"

"Ah, that's why no one told me," she said. "Trage
doesn't take on me, you know, I have no gift for it, I ha
only to lay a finger on one and it falls flat. Tragedies a
not so common as they were last year — they wanted to sa
theirs from me."

Galen made a gesture of astonishment. "And you did
hear anything, either, about the arrests?"

This startled her. "What arrests? It isn't true abo
the students?" She looked at him. "What has happened

"No one knows. But I'm told that several people ha
been denounced to the French authorities."

Anna tried to stand up. "Paul, I don't feel well," s
said inaudibly.

He pressed her back in her chair, looking into her fa
"What's the matter, my love? You've been over-worki
and not eating enough. Come now, you must eat." Wi
the greatest gentleness, he held a morsel of food to h
mouth and watched her while she swallowed it. "Tha
better."

Lotte had been looking at Marie with a furtive exciteme
The way that Paul was playing with her roused and delight
all her malice, she could not help joining in.

" Did you say someone had been denounced ? " she asked.

" The whole thing is rumour," Galen said slowly. " But — they say that one of the English politicians was shot last night."

Marie was startled into crying out. " But they didn't come ! "

He looked at her and said, " Ah, you heard that, did you ? "

She had controlled herself quickly. " I heard something about it in the chemist's — but they all chatter so."

" And you're too good to listen to chatter," Lotte jeered.

" Not in the least." She smiled. " In my village we heard all the gossip at breakfast, from our servant ; she was a sister-in-law of a cousin of the postmistress, so of course she knew everything."

" My dear Lotte," Galen said, " you make life very hard for Marie — and she has no other friend here of her age."

Lotte felt a just rage. " Oh, hasn't she ! She has the English officer. . . ." She checked herself, and added slyly, " I haven't seen him today, he must be tired of amusing himself."

The undertone of cruel amusement in Lotte's voice made Marie uneasy. She was used to the other young woman's malice, the malice of a schoolgirl, she could ward it off easily, but this was new. She and Paul know something they are keeping from me, she thought. Her attention was distracted by Anna, who had become leaden in colour and was leaning over the table with her elbow on it — surely the first time she had dared to put her elbow on the table during a meal, in front of her mother. Her husband was bending towards her, and he pressed between her lips a piece of roll she tried feebly to reject.

" Eat, my dear — it's what you need," Galen said. But he gave it up, and said casually to Marie, " So you heard them talking in the village about an attempted assassination ? "

Now she knew what they were hiding from her. Paul believes I gave them away, she thought. For a moment she felt only terror. The effort she made to appear calm really calmed her, and she was able to say quietly,

" No, I didn't. It was you who said that."

Galen looked at her severely. " You're quite mistaken. It's not a word I should use. I believe that an Englishman was in fact shot in Mainz, last night or this morning. But it was an accident."

She thought coldly : You don't catch me that way. " Are there any Englishmen in Mainz ? "

" So it seems."

Another moment of panic seized her, and before she could stop herself she had cried, " Why are you all watching me ? " She controlled herself again at once. " Oh, I see, you're wondering why I've altered my hair—" she touched it, drawing out a curl on her finger — " My sister and I did our hair like this for parties — always : we promised each other when I left that we would do it any day we felt divinely happy."

This was true.

Lotte said maliciously, " And what's divine about today, I'd like to know ? "

" It's the day I gave up trying to be noble and sentimental, and became my deceitful French self," she said lightly.

" You do well to give up pretending to be German," her mother-in-law said.

" Perhaps," Lotte cried, " she expected to be English next."

" I'm quite sure," Galen said gravely, " that Marie has been discretion itself. In any case, since the English officer isn't here any longer, I needn't warn her against him."

There was nothing in his voice to account for the sudden anguish she felt.

" Has he gone ? " she asked.

Paul von Galen looked at her. " Surely you knew that he went into Mainz yesterday evening ? He went instead of the French officers. There were people waiting outside the railway station, and some sort of row must have started."

She felt nothing. . . . Do you know what it is like, to feel nothing ? It is first of all an agony.

" There was a row ? "

" So I'm told. But—" he smiled — " don't expect me to know whether, as the postman says, at least a hundred people were killed, or, according to the stationmaster as reported by young Gauss, only one. I don't even know whether it was a bomb chucked into Captain Long's car that killed him, or if he were shot in the back, as another version says. The only certain thing is that he's dead."

After that, it is a trembling of the whole body, without any pain : the body is the first to understand. She repeated quietly, " Dead ? "

" Probably someone had intended to take pot-shots at the Englishmen who didn't come."

" You knew," she said.

" What did I know ? " Galen asked — in the indulgent voice of one humouring an invalid. " I daresay someone warned the French. It was like them not to go themselves, when there was danger."

Let me get away, she thought blindly. She half rose, holding on to the table. " Yes, of course. Yes——"
Quite simply — since it was all now clear and simple — she said, " I was too late."

Galen stood up.

" I thought so. You warned the French."

" Marie ! " Anna groaned.

Marie spoke to her reassuringly. " Don't worry, Anna, nothing matters." She smiled at her brother-in-law. " Yes, I warned them. You knew that, too."

" No," he said. " I only guessed. You can be satisfied with yourself. If you had said nothing, Captain Long would have stayed here on duty. He would be alive now."

Bertha von Leyde interrupted him. " I ought to have expected some such vileness from a Frenchwoman," she said emotionally. " Thank God Johann didn't live long enough for you to deceive him with other men. I would never have believed it."

Marie had become calm, calm. Although her body was trembling still, she felt detached from it, and her only naked feeling was that she must show nothing to her enemies. " Are you sure you weren't prepared for a simple little adultery — at least ? " she said in a light voice.

" You'd have done better to go on making eyes at the major," Lotte cried. " He may be a little defective, but he's alive ! "

Marie looked slowly and deliberately into all their faces — except into Anna's. Anna had buried her face in her hands and did not look up. Her glance reached Heinrich : he had not spoken since she came into the room, and he was, she saw, very pale. He stared back at her, with defiance.

" Don't try any of your lies on me," he said loudly. " No one here will believe you."

She said softly, " My poor child."

Galen called the scene to order with a dignified gesture of his long hand. " Come, this is far too serious for any personal feeling — it's not a family quarrel. Marie — I must use an ugly word — is a traitor, she has betrayed us, at least once that we know of ; and she must be prevented from doing it again."

" You came here without being invited," Bertha said, rolling her lips over the words, " we welcomed you — and this is how you repay our kindness and trust. By selling us to these thieves."

" But what else did you expect," Marie said, " of a Frenchwoman ? "

" Marie is quite right," Galen said quickly. " She can't help behaving according to her nature and her upbringing. She is an alien element here. This doesn't excuse her, it's only a reason to eliminate her and her natural duplicity."

He had pressed lightly on the last few words. She noticed it, and for the first time she felt contempt for him, and a quiver of excitement.

" You must know all about the nature of duplicity, Paul. I suppose you treated Colonel Maulnier to at least one of your speeches about friendship and the need to make peace, and the rest ! "

" Are you doubting my sincerity ? " he said mildly. " What I say I mean."

" And at the same time you were plotting this murder," she smiled. " I congratulate you on your sincerity."

Galen looked at her, raising his eyebrows. " My dear girl, nothing could be a better proof of my sincere dis-interest. It is absolutely necessary to the peace of the world that France and Germany should be allies. If necessary, we must force our friendship on France. To do that we must be strong. It follows, perfectly logically, that we must make Germany irresistible. . . ." He stopped. " You are a woman, you are not used to logic," he said, smiling.

The spiritual horror of his sincerity broke on her. " You are insane," she said, with a great effort.

" It's quite usual," Galen said calmly, " to say that a man who knows his own mind is insane — until he succeeds. Then he becomes a leader. I'm satisfied."

The baroness had been listening with a baffled face, her mouth working. " Paul, this is no time to be, what is it ?, disinterested," she said harshly. " Get rid of her. Pack her off to the French. It's all she's fit for."

" Even they don't want her," Lotte cried.

Marie looked at her with smiling indifference. " It's true — I have no country. . . . That's better than one you have to serve by lying and murder."

" You're very clever," Lotte said bitterly. " But what good is your cleverness ? You call yourself patriotic — you haven't even had a child."

" Be quiet, Lotte." Galen sat down again at the table, facing Marie. He had seated himself next his son. As he talked he looked into her face, like a patient tutor trying to help a dense pupil. " Marie, a great deal depends — for you — on the way you answer the questions I'm going to put to you. You've always seemed a reasonable human being. Try to be one now."

" If it's reasonable to see a difference between patriotism and murder I am reasonable," she said.

" I congratulate you," he said drily. " And if you can also see a difference between a vindictive peace and war your sight is better than mine. . . . Marie, my dear, this won't help you. Are you going to listen to me ? "

It was impossible to doubt his good faith. He is possessed, she thought.

" I'm listening."

" You didn't find it out yourself, you had an informant. Who is it ? "

She was silent.

" I'll be frank with you," Galen went on. " Your

omfort — more than that — depends on your telling the
ruth."

She could see Heinrich without turning her head. The
boy had drawn himself a little away from his father : his
thin body was rigid, his hands clenched resting on the edge
of the table. She looked at these poor hands, at the marks
on them of last winter's chilblains, with pity.

" I had no informant."

Heinrich fell back in his chair, he grew small and limp.
" What did I say ? " — he drew in a long noisy breath —
" She listens at keyholes."

" My dear child, why should I listen at keyholes ? " she
said gently. " It's quite the stupidest way of spying."

Anna took her hands from her face, and looked at him.

" You would do any mean trick," he shouted. " Anything. You're a — a harlot."

" Heinrich," his mother whispered, " be careful."

He took no notice of her. " She is a harlot. You are !
You went with both of them — the French officer as well.
Yes, and you tried to bribe me. Here's your book."

He dragged the Ronsard from his pocket and threw it
on the table in front of her.

" What are you talking about, Heinrich ? " his father said
sharply.

Anna smiled like an idiot. She leaned across the table
and pulled at her husband's arm. " Dear Paul, since the
Englishmen didn't come after all, why must we have all
this fuss ? . . . And I really must go and see what old
Gregor is doing. You know, he's had another of his
visions this morning : he says we must expect the Kaiser
any day now . . . and what with his mania for saluting
every time I give him an order, we get nothing done. You
really must speak to him. . . ."

" For heaven's sake, Anna," Galen said without kindness,

" keep Gregor and his visions to a more suitable moment Have you no sense of responsibility ? "

" My good Anna, you are a fool," Bertha von Leyde said contemptuously.

Anna leaned back in her chair. Her forehead, that high sloping forehead with its perpetually raised eyebrows, was wet : she wiped it with the side of her hand, furtively She was still, Marie saw, afraid, and she did not move her eyes from her son's face.

Galen, his head lying on one side, was saying quietly " Well, Marie, you realise that you are making it impossible for me to protect you."

" But how good of you to have had such a thought," she mocked him.

" If you'd been willing to help us by explaining exactly how you were able to spy for the French I might persuade my — my immediate superiors to be lenient. For once."

" And no doubt I could spy on the French for you ! "

" That would be possible," he said.

" I would rather die," she said with a sudden calm anger He shrugged his shoulders. " How romantic you are Marie. You surprise me. . . . You may find it harder than you think."

He had spoken very quietly and amiably, but she felt a shock in the centre of her body — as though she had put her hand on a branch laid on a stone and felt the snake move. She forced herself to say soberly, " I'm not afraid of dying, Paul. It's not very amusing here, you know."

Galen stood up, with a grimace of pain. " Think it over until this evening, my dear Marie," he said gently " and tell me then. You understand me quite well, though you're pretending not to. I mean just what I say — an untrustworthy member of the family — " he smiled at her as though she would appreciate the joke — " must be eliminated. I shall do anything I can to make it easy for you, I dislike hurting people, but don't deceive yourself, this is a serious affair, not one of the comedies you enjoy playing."

" My poor Paul," she said easily, " don't count on me for a tragic part. I shall ruin your little scene."

She watched his long stooping body cross the room slowly to the door into the main wing. The heavy key was on this side : he locked it, and came back with the key — and gave it to his mother-in-law. " Mamma, you had better keep this. I can't trust my wife not to lose it."

" Where are you going ? " Bertha asked heavily.

" I must see Altdorf and get back here before dark. I ought to be with him now." He paused on his way to the other door. " You won't any of you be able to leave the house," he said reflectively, " I shall lock the outer door as I go. . . . There is no need for anyone to sit here with Marie. In fact, I want her to be alone. . . . You can go to your own rooms. Lotte, leave the door of your bedroom open, so that you will hear her if she tries to leave this room. Keep Heinrich with you, Anna."

He turned to Marie. In a polite friendly voice, polite host to guest, he said, " You look cold. Are you ? " He touched her. " No. . . . But you're trembling."

He had reached the door before one of them spoke. It was Bertha.

" And how is Anna to cook the supper if she is to stay in her room ? "

He turned with his hand on the door, and smiled at her kindly. " We'll see about that when I come back, Mamma."

He went out. They heard his footsteps along the passage to the outer door, and the grinding sound of the lock, then complete silence. Marie felt that she would collapse, she pulled herself together with the effort she made not to move.

And not to think. What good was it to think? Later, at the very last minute, she would think of Adrian and he would help her: now, she had to keep quiet, to smile, and above all, not to make a fuss. And Anna, she thought, I must make it easy for Anna . . . poor Anna.

" Help me to my room, Lotte," Bertha said.

She watched her mother-in-law go out, leaning all her weight on Lotte's narrow shoulder. Then she turned, smiling, to Anna. Anna was not looking at her. She was looking at her son.

" It was you told her," she said quietly.

" I never did," Heinrich shouted. " It's a lie."

" My little love," Anna murmured, " I know you did." She half smiled, her tragic laughable smile. " Why, it's written on your forehead."

The boy lifted his hand quickly, to cover the writing on his forehead. His poor face seemed to be breaking up. " I didn't mean it, mother. I don't know why I did it. I didn't mean anything. . . ." His voice, too, broke down. " Oh, what can we do? Whatever can we do? You won't tell him, will you? "

" It wasn't his fault, Anna," Marie said.

Her sister-in-law looked at her as though she were a stranger. " You have made it harder for him to live here."

" I have ? "

Gentle and implacable, Anna repeated, " Yes, you, Marie."

" Let's go now, mother," Heinrich stammered. He pulled at her arm. She did not move at once.

" There's something I've always wanted to tell you, Heinrich," she said softly. " It was me — it was my arms and hands got burned pulling your wooden horse out of the stove. Not your father's. . . . You knew all about it when it happened, and then you forgot it was me. Why did you forget, my one ? "

" I don't know," Heinrich muttered. He was crying now bitterly : tears fell on his hands and he looked at them as though he thought it must be raining.

" Come, don't cry," his mother said gently, trying, but in vain, to hide her happiness. The boy flung himself into her arms, and clung to her, still weeping. " Come," she said.

As they went out, Marie could not help crying softly, " Anna ! "

But Anna ignored her. . . . The door closed, she was alone. For a moment she stood and let the full bitterness of Anna's desertion rise through her, from her heart to her tongue — it had a salt taste, and it revived her. She lifted her hands, lightly, and dropped them, a gesture of contempt and amusement. She looked round. How absurd, she thought deliberately, to be spending my last hour or hours in a German kitchen. She walked about the room, touching a chair, the table, a cup, with the curiosity of a child. A cup, she said to herself : a chair. Taking a flower from the bowl on the table, she stood in front of the mirror to fasten it in her dress. She was doing this when the door opened and Bertha von Leyde came in. The old lady's cheeks were congested and swollen, as when she was in one of her rages ; her lips moved, but no words came out. Marie decided to speak.

" Have you left something ? " she said gently. " I'm glad you came, I wanted to ask you to forgive me for marrying Johann. He was happy with me, but that meant nothing to you at the time and it means nothing now. You wanted something for the future. Forgive me. Now I understand why. It's when you can't look forward to any future that it becomes precious. . . ." She hesitated, surprised by what she had just said. Until she said it, she had not known it. And it was true. " Will you forgive me ? "

Bertha took no notice. She walked slowly to the other door, the door leading to the French wing, and unlocked it with the key she took out of the pocket of her under-skirt.

" Go," she said drily, " go and beg of your country-men."

She went back to the other door and went out, without glancing at the young woman. Alone again, Marie ran to the main door. She had her hand on it, and in the same instant she saw herself standing in front of the French colonel — and in front of Major Aubrac — asking them to save her. A revulsion — of pride or shame, she could not have told which — seized her, and she turned away and walked back to the table, slowly, and sat down. I don't want to live, she thought. As she thought it, she knew that it was a lie, but for the moment it suited her better than the truth. She was tired. I am tired, she repeated. And that was a lie, too.

She had her back to both doors, and she did not hear the smaller door open, very slowly and softly, blunt short fingers gripping the handle so that it turned noiselessly. Before she heard her, Lotte was in the middle of the room, close to her. . . .

" Why have you come, Lotte ? " she asked her quietly.

The girl looked at her with hatred. " Why shouldn't I ? . . . I came to look at you."

This was a little amusing. " Well ? What do you see ? "

" Selfish, useless," Lotte said fiercely, " absolutely use-less. You ought not to be alive. All you want is to have an easy life, it's all you think of, how you can be gay and amuse yourself. I've no patience with you."

" How glad you must be to have something to accuse

me of — something serious. Serious enough to take in the
one thing you don't, you can't ever forgive me."

" What do you mean ? "

" That I know how to be happy ! "

" It isn't that ! " Lotte had turned scarlet ; her clear
skin showed every change in her mood. " It's your awful
meanness," she shouted. " You're like a peasant. You're
hopelessly material, you haven't an atom of idealism or
nobility . . . you can't feel. . . ."

Marie smiled. " Now I truly don't know what you mean,
Lotte. I was carefully brought up, my mother and all
my teachers told me I ought to be ashamed when I had
made anything, even a kitchen chair, feel that it was not
being a success. If that's what you mean by material, or
if it's material to want to be polite to things, to like this
table for being a table, and not a copy of the Place Kleber
in Strasbourg, and the sun for being the sun, and you,
yes, you, Lotte, for being what you are, a good little German,
hard but not nearly so hard as you think, an awful liar,
impatient, jealous, and loyal and very very brave — yes, all
right then, I'm a materialist."

" I hate you," Lotte said.

" Not nearly so deeply as you envy me," Marie said
softly.

She watched the other girl walk to the door leading to
the main wing, look at it for a second, try it. It opened.
Closing it again, Lotte turned round quickly.

" Who unlocked it ? "

Marie was silent.

" Mamma did, of course," the girl said scornfully. " She
has the key. . . . She's even softer than I thought she was."

" You needn't do anything or make any fuss. I'm not
going to run away."

Lotte ran back to the table. " You fool ! The larder

key fits this door — " she held her hand out, with a key in it — " I came in to unlock it."

Marie felt something that was almost grief. " Why Lotte ? "

" Go," Lotte said, " go, go. Go and be happy. Run away. Hop it."

" Why do you want to save me ? " Marie asked quietly. She stood up. She and Lotte were of a height. They looked at each other, the nervous fury of the one so close to the other's smiling serenity that they touched. They were only separated by a frontier, an imaginary line, very highly charged.

" I want to get rid of you," Lotte said. She hesitated. " No, you fool — it isn't that. . . . We ought to be able to understand each other. You're not any older than I am. . . . I can't go away, Richard and I are both caught, we shall never escape. But you might."

" I don't think so," Marie said. " We're all caught." Yes, it was grief. She smiled. " If I were sorry for the world I should have to be sorry for myself — and that would be rather disgraceful."

" Hurry," Lotte said.

" Why should I go ? What could I do ? "

" Get married. Yes, have a son — I'll tell mine not to hate him. . . . Perhaps."

Marie wanted to throw her arms up, she wanted to cry out, and instead she said quietly, " You must ! "

" Perhaps," Lotte repeated obstinately.

Suddenly they fell into each other's arms ; they embraced fiercely and awkwardly, like children, and only for a second. Lotte pushed her away. " Only go now," she said, " do go. Before I detest you again."

She ran out of the room, but shut the door carefully without a sound.

Marie made a gesture of complete indifference. She sat down again, and without knowing what she was doing said in a low voice, " No ! " In almost the same moment she heard a light sound at the other side of the main door — a footstep, was it ? She sprang to her feet. And listened. There was a knock, and she felt a flame of joy, surely it was a flame ?, leap through her.

" Come in."

The door was already opening. As he came in Aubrac looked at her, he saw the change in her face.

" I see you know," he said.

The truth, why not tell the truth ? " When you knocked, I thought there had been a mistake, it wasn't true."

Aubrac's face twitched. " Really ? . . . I'm sorry."

" You came to tell me," she said politely. " That was good of you. Very good. . . . You must hate me."

" Not at all," he answered drily.

In a curious way she had felt at her ease from the moment he began talking. She realised, suddenly, that for the first time he was speaking to her in French. He must be ill, she thought. But he was not whiter than usual, and his mutilated hands did not shake so much.

" No, of course not," she said quickly. " You feel only contempt. . . . To hate someone, even a young woman as worthless and careless as I am, you must feel at least a little respect for her."

" You can respect for her courage a young woman you dislike for her inexcusable, her atrocious — crime," he said slowly. " Listen, Marie, I came——"

She interrupted him. " What did you say ? "

" What is the matter ? "

" Nothing," she said hurriedly, " nothing."

He went on in a coldly formal voice. " Colonel Maulnier has decided to arrest your brother-in-law. You will probably be in some danger. He has been able to arrange for you to go back to France — to your family. You will be given a passport."

She thanked him, politely, and briefly. There was a silence.

" You don't want to go ? " he said at last.

She shook her head, confused. " Will you answer a question ? Why did you bother about me ? "

" It was purely a matter of form." With a sharp movement, he came nearer to her. " Are you afraid of your family ? Or simply afraid to go back to France ? "

She stood up. She was again at the end of her strength. " Please go away," she said sternly.

" What's the matter ? " He checked himself with a stiff gesture of one arm. " Forgive me. You're suffering . . . I've been clumsy."

Marie felt that she could bear anything from him except gentleness. She defended herself by mocking him. " Why do you imagine that I feel anything — except disappointment ? I'm obviously incapable of the proper feelings. Everything I do proves it. . . . And in fact I scarcely feel grateful for your kindness, it's too much to put up with."

He did not answer her at once. She had time to think that defeat and the refusal of defeat had given Frenchmen this look of contempt and endurance, as though the man were being mocked by his skeleton, as though, reduced to its skeleton, France were seen to be made of something harder than bone.

" I didn't arrange anything," he said. " Neither did Colonel Maulnier. It was arranged for us by some senator or president, or a banker — to please your father. Your father — Dr. Jouvenet — he must have been delighted to hear of your marriage — is a brave man. He was what we used to call a resister. You wouldn't know the word.

. . . If he wanted your passport, he had the right to ask
for it. We've been ordered to send you home. . . . Along
with the instructions there was a letter from your father
to the colonel."

Before she could stifle it, Marie's cry had given her away.
She turned from him and sat down, determined not to give
him the satisfaction of disappointing her. " Did he send
any message for me ? " she asked calmly.

" Did you expect one ? "

She was silent.

" Yes. . . . Your sister is married — she has married
an American officer, and she is going to America to his
parents——"

She interrupted him — with astonishment, and a light
anguish. " Suzanne married ? Married and going away ?
It's impossible. Why, she knows everyone in the village,
she belongs to them . . . when we were in Normandy she
used to lie awake in the early morning and remember everything, every single sound, that was going on at home — the
milk-girl, the postman, even the goats. . . . And she's very
silent and cautious. Not like me."

Aubrac had picked up the Ronsard lying on the table.
He turned the pages, with a look of irony, and put it
down.

" Except for a family habit of marrying foreigners," he
observed. " I daresay I'm prejudiced against Americans.
. . . You'll be able to go there with her."

It is so much easier to defend oneself against insults
than against kindness. She smiled in his face. " To
America — where no one knows me, and no one will look
at me derisively and say : There's Marie Jouvenet, she
married a Boche during the war, she has a Boche name of
some sort. . . . I shall escape all the penalties of my — my
error."

" Exactly."

" Do you know that you have been speaking to me in French ? " she said, smiling.

He was taken aback. " I'd forgotten——"

" What ? "

" That you don't understand French."

She should have been able to laugh at this, but she was seized by a frightful rage : she no longer felt any humility before him, she felt only anger and a longing to strike him. She was trembling, but she forced herself to stand up, and to look at his face.

" I understand yours very well," she said.

They stared at each other like bitter enemies. A strange grief crossed Aubrac's face. He took a step back, and said in a formal voice.

" I should be glad if you'd make your mind up. . . . Either you come now, or not at all."

All her anger left her, and she felt ashamed. She knew that she was going to let him save her — it would be absurd to insist on dying. Absurd and exaggerated. Very well — since I have decided to live, the least I can do, she thought, is to live politely.

" Do you realise that your own people, this time, are offering you the chance to run away ? " Aubrac said ironically. " You can bolt with a clear conscience."

" It would embarrass my father to have me at home."

" Of course. . . . The least you can do for him is to go to America."

" There are milk-girls and postmen in America — I suppose," she said, smiling. " And rivers. . . . The Loire isn't the only river in the world. . . ."

There was a silence.

" Good," he said after a moment, in a dry voice. " I can give you five minutes to collect anything you want to take. Provided you can take it without being noticed. Hurry, please."

She shook her head. "Nothing. There's nothing I want to take. Nothing here belongs to me."

"Really?" He picked up the Ronsard. "What about this?"

"No."

He looked round the room. Limping over to the mantel-piece, he took down the miniature and held it out to her. "This?"

She shook her head again.

"Why not?"

She was able to speak lightly. "You must be enjoying yourself. . . . I can't take either of them. One of them belongs utterly to France, and the other — you should hear my mother-in-law on it, her tongue is nearly as sharp as yours — the other belongs in the country where he was born, and learned to invade other countries and to be gentle and honest and to die young. . . . Both countries have rejected me — I can't take anything that belongs to them."

"And you? . . . Do you reject both of them?"

What a question! She showed him her hands, empty, and let them drop at her side. "I haven't a country."

He came close to her. "Really?" he said, watching her with what, in a less distorted face, would have been kindness. She read it as cruelty. "Are you sure? Not even in the early morning? When you are half asleep, and you close your eyes again and see the pigeon walk across the yard. . . . Do you imagine you'll see that in America? I suppose your sister's husband is rich, all Americans are — you'll be very comfortable."

She would not defend herself any longer. Not because she was tired, or had forgotten how foolish it is to show

that you have been hurt, to show anguish. But because she
had just, in this very moment, realised something that
made the idea of defending herself seem the most foolish
thing in the world. You can defend yourself against so
little in life that it is not worth the enormous trouble.
Against the real enemies in a life — against the cruelty of
human beings for each other, and against their kindness,
and against the pain of loss, against the cold that follows
a death — no defence is good, even mockery is no good.

"I'd rather be the poorest servant-girl in Berthenay."

"So you have a country?"

"Yes, of course . . . my country is derision and
penalties."

Still watching her, Aubrac said, "I have another offer.
. . . My sister has charge of a houseful of children without
parents or relatives, some of them have been running wild,
others were wounded, some are cripples. There is very
little money, my sister and her helpers cook, scrub, mend,
nurse — they nurse more than broken bodies. These
children learned hate and fear too young . . . that's the
German poison, not their guns, not their bombs. That's
their unforgivable sin. . . ." His voice changed, becoming light and mocking. "Heaven forbid Colonel von
Galen should find out that I take him seriously — at least
once a year for a moment. . . ." He hesitated and said
harshly, "That's my offer. Take it or leave it."

"Are you making it to Marie Jouvenet or to Marie von
Leyde?" she asked.

"To both."

After a long silence — she knew what she was going to
do, but she had first of all to humble herself as she had
not done since she was a child — she said, "I accept it
for both of them——"

"Wait a moment," he interrupted. "Do you mind

broken finger-nails and an aching back ? " He looked at
her body and stretched his hand to it, a gesture that in
another would have been longing.

" You'll see how easily I stand such things," she said
drily.

" There'll be other hardships. You'll be distrusted —
perhaps always. The other women will know who you
are."

" I can bear that, too," she said, smiling, " I'm never
sorry for myself." Her self-control broke suddenly. " Do
you think they can say worse than you've said to me ?
Or do you think anything worse can happen to me, after
today ? " Aubrac put his hand out again ; she thought he
was going to touch her, and evaded him — " No, don't
soften towards me, I dislike it as much as I detest for-
giveness. I don't want anyone to forgive me — you least
of all. As for your sister—" she stopped abruptly : no
use pretending that she did not care what women who would
know only by looking at her that she was ashamed thought
of her — " Do you think your sister will hate me ? "

" I'll take you to her myself."

She could not help a gesture of revulsion.

" You ? "

" I'm going home this evening on leave. . . . Do you
dislike the idea of travelling with me ? "

" No," she said, trembling.

She had no idea why she was trembling — unless it was
her obscure sense that she was involving her life with his
in a way neither of them intended, and that in their life
together she would meet and be forced to answer all the
questions she had so far and with the help of exile, disgrace,
death, evaded. It was so obscure that she did not understand it, she was only afraid, and — because she was afraid
— she smiled as though she knew that from now on the

worst things she would have to face were chilblains and a pain in the back.

" What did you say ? " Aubrac asked.

She made an effort to speak calmly. " Yes. . . . Yes, of course I'll come with you."

" After all, you're not a coward," he said slowly.

" And not absolutely useless or hideous," she mocked him. Her voice changed. " Do you think I shan't know how to defend myself ? " she said simply. " After all, I'm a Frenchwoman. . . . I'm not an idiot. I've humiliated myself farther than anyone — even you — can humiliate me. And I've lost everything—" she felt a terrible weakness and grief : he tried to catch her as she swayed — and for the second time she avoided him — " everything . . . but you'll see . . . I shall be polite."

" I'm sure of it," he said. He went painfully to the door. Turning when he had opened it, he saw that she was looking at the room. " Come, Marie," he said gently.

She walked towards him quickly and lightly, and out of the room.

2

Some time later — it was still daylight outside, and a good hour before curfew, but the room, lighted only from the skylight, was beginning to darken — the other door, the door leading to the yard and the servants' bedrooms — opened. Leaning on Heinrich's shoulder, Bertha stood there and looked round the room before she came in.

" You see, I was right," she said slowly. " She *has* gone."

They came into the room. The boy held his narrow shoulders stiffly under the pressure of his grandmother's and : he fitted his steps to hers, with a little air of patience, which belonged to an older person — it belonged in fact to his mother, and this was the first time he had used it : you would have said it had been born with him.

" I'm glad she's gone," he said quietly.

Bertha took her hand from his shoulder : he saw the Ronsard lying on the table and seized it.

" What is it ? " Bertha asked. She took it from him. " Some rubbishy French book," she said, with contempt. She kept it and moved towards the stove.

The boy hurried after her. " Don't burn it, grand-mamma, I want it."

The old woman looked at him. " Why do you want it ? Because it was hers, I suppose."

" No," he said soberly, " I don't care about that, I want to read it."

" It will do you no good," she said drily.

Opening the stove, she threw it in. He hesitated for a moment, then thrust his hand into the stove and snatched the book out, unharmed. His grandmother did not say anything. She made a gesture, unaccustomed, of fatigue and indifference, and let him take the book to the table : he sat down there and began turning the pages. She watched him for a minute.

It was growing darker in the room. Soon there would be no light at all, and he was straining his eyes. She lit the oil lamp they used here, and carried it to the table, placing it so that the circle of weak light fell on the book. She looked with a little anxiety at Heinrich. He was frown-ing, and he did not look up. " I don't understand it very well," he confessed, " there's something here about the light, *lumière*, you know ; I should like to read it to you, but we'd better wait, hadn't we ? "

His grandmother put his hand on his shoulder again.

She wanted to tell him that she could not wait very long, she would not be here long, but, a door opening, an outer door, and sending a current of cold air into the room, she helped him instead, in silence, to push the book into his pocket.

August–December 1944

THE END

Printed in Great Britain by R. & R. CLARK, LIMITED, *Edinburgh*